D1798226

Eating the Big Fish

Young David was the only champion Israel could muster against the might of the giant, Goliath. We know the unlikely end of that confrontation. The scales seem even more heavily tilted against the three young Jews, two men and a woman, who decide that the only way to ensure the safety of the modern state of Israel is to overthrow the foreign minister of a friendly power, the effect of whose policies the three conspirators feel sure must edge Israel towards destruction.

How can three ordinary people secretly topple a political colossus? Their plan is to take a hostage of such enormous value to the American government that they will then be able to bargain from strength. But once they go into action they find themselves caught up in a growing storm of violence, intrigue and deception. The story mounts to a climax which is bound to astonish the reader. By the end of the book, he may well also find himself wondering whether events like those described here have not actually happened already. Certainly, none of the news he reads each day will ever seem quite so straightforward again. He may even come to doubt the official version of what happened between David and Goliath in that valley at Elah long ago!

by the same author

Fiction

THE LAST DAYS
THE KNIFEMAN
THE REAPERS
STAG BOY
THE BAREBONES
THE WORLD TURNED UPSIDE-DOWN
BIG MISTER
THE BLOODY AFFRAY AT RIVERSIDE DRIVE
THE TRAIL TO BEAR PAW MOUNTAIN
A WEEKEND WITH CAPTAIN JACK
THE DAY OF CHAMINUKA

Non-Fiction

THE TRIBE AND ITS SUCCESSORS

Eating
the Big Fish

WILLIAM RAYNER

COLLINS
St James's Place London
1977

William Collins Sons & Co Ltd
London · Glasgow · Sydney · Auckland
Toronto · Johannesburg

First published 1977
© William Rayner 1977
ISBN 0 00 222208 6
Set in Intertype Baskerville
Made and printed in Great Britain by
William Collins Sons & Co Ltd Glasgow

To Simon who helped

1

The Boeing came in through the misty sunlight of an October morning : a big gleaming apparition, amazing yet utterly commonplace. It touched down on the runway and taxied to a halt. The first flight of the day from New York had arrived at Heathrow. Passengers disembarked and made their way through Customs. The journey had been uneventful.

The young man in the airport lounge attracted no attention. He looked like one of the new generation of executives. His dark hair was somewhat longer than would once have been thought proper, but the hair was stylishly cut. The black line of his moustache stretched down below the corners of his mouth, but the moustache was well trimmed. Though his suit was a sober grey, his pink shirt gave a hint of extravagance. He seemed a typical young businessman of today. He was carrying a briefcase and had a copy of *The Times* tucked under his arm.

When he heard the New York flight announced, the young man made his way into the Reception Hall. He waited, brown eyes scanning the crowd, but nobody looked at him for more than a moment. He saw lovers reunited, tourists being gathered by their courier, a grey-haired woman overcome by tears as she welcomed the big, embarrassed man who might have been her son. He watched the two officials greet Professor Morrell, noted the handshakes and exchange of courtesies, his eyes following these things without any show of interest. The three of them made their way towards the exit. When they got near him, the young man turned his head, looking beyond them, as if in search of the colleague he had been sent to meet. As he did so, his grip tightened upon the handle of his briefcase.

A black stud set in the folds of the leather blinked once. The Professor and his companions went on towards their official car. The young executive stood in the Hall a little longer. Finally he gave a shake of the head and turned away. It seemed as if the colleague he had been sent to meet had failed to make the flight after all.

There were only a few casual spectators when Professor Morrell arrived at the American Embassy in Grosvenor Square. The Press was not in evidence. The bystanders watched the Ambassador come out to welcome the Professor on the paved area at the top of the steps. What they saw was two big men, flanked by officials, standing in the misty sunlight, pumping each other's hands, smiling and nodding under the outspread wings of the gilded eagle.

Among these bystanders was a girl. She was about twenty-two years old, slightly built, her figure muffled in a long coat. A pretty girl, her dark eyebrows a surprising contrast to her corn-blonde hair. Although she had paused to watch the meeting, her eyes betrayed only the vaguest curiosity. After a moment she re-slung her shoulder-bag, twisting the clasp shut. A black stud blinked in a fold of the leather. The girl wandered off across the square, past the statue of President Roosevelt, who at that moment had a seagull perched on his head. Professor Morrell was ushered inside the Embassy building.

Later that day Professor Arthur Morrell left the Embassy. He was on his way to keep an appointment with his old friend Doctor Haltrecht of University College, and he had chosen to go on foot so as to renew his acquaintance with the streets of Central London. He had known these streets before, first as a young GI, a corporal of infantry, twenty years old, and not at all sure that he would make it to twenty-one, his perceptions sharpened by the death that might well await him across the Channel. A few years later he had again spent some time in London, during his vacations from Oxford. London reminded him of the two people he had once been: the soldier, little more than a boy, and the diligent research student. It reminded him of being young and vulnerable, obscure and uncertain of his future. Professor Morrell wanted to indulge these memories and he knew you could not do that from the back seat of a taxi. You had to walk.

He strolled along Duke Street and joined the crowds of shoppers in Oxford Street, looking about him reminiscently. He was not quite at ease, though. The walk was robbed of some of its pleasure because he knew the man would be somewhere at hand, the stocky balding agent in the brown overcoat. His bodyguard! The idea struck Professor Morrell as both unlikely and distasteful. He wanted to regard himself in the same light as he had always done : a scientist devoted to research, leading a life that was happily removed from the worlds of politics and violence. Of course, he recognized intellectually that things had changed. His discoveries and the techniques he was now pioneering were vitally important, not only to science and medicine but also to national security and the defence of the state. He recognized this, but he resented having to do so. He felt he had been thrust into an ambiguous moral position. As a scientist, he knew his integrity was being jeopardized, but as a man of patriotic instincts he had come to the conclusion that he must co-operate, particularly after it was pointed out to him that his published findings were enough to set Russian micro-biologists hard on the same trail. From now on, scientists from the power blocs of the world would be engaged in a secret race, and it was his duty to ensure that the race would be won for America and her allies. This awareness had driven him to take on certain work, work with fearful implications, work that was being carried on even now in his laboratories. He consoled himself with the idea that these researches were meant only for the defence of America. He had been given that assurance by the Pentagon, though sometimes he found himself wondering whether the generals and politicians could be trusted to keep their word. In any case, as he was uneasily aware, you could not draw any genuine line of demarcation. There was no real difference.

It all depended on how the knowledge gained was used.

He thought of the atomic physicists of the early nineteen-forties, whose brilliant work had culminated in the holocaust of Hiroshima, and wondered how they felt at the moment of their success.

Professor Morrell was not yet used to his new eminence. He knew the importance of his findings, but all the same he had been bowled over by the sudden recognition granted him by the scientific world. Although it had meant leaving Judith, he had felt really good when the news arrived that his old university of Oxford wished to confer an honorary degree on him. 'Outstanding advances in the field of micro-biology.' That was acceptable. That was the kind of celebrity he understood, a tribute by fellow scientists, a great moment, a crown to one's career.

Morrell was not the chilly, rational figure that journalists and writers of fiction have projected over the years as the stereotype of the scientist. He was at least as much in need of admiration and love as the rest of mankind. Perhaps more than most, he had always wanted applause – from his family, from his teachers, and from his colleagues in the world of science – and now that he had won it, he felt something deeper than satisfaction, something more like a profound relief. Arthur Morrell was sometimes uncomfortably aware of the lack of certainty planted deep in his nature.

Perhaps that was why throughout his career he had turned to women as well as to science, seeking reassurance from both. Nor was it any accident that Professor Morrell adopted a naïve simplicity in his intimate dealings with women. His affaires were a source of sly amusement to his colleagues, he knew that. Behind his back they called him 'Stud Morrell'. My God, he thought, was that how they saw him? The reality was very different. This old-style profligate, five foot eleven in his socks, one hundred and ninety pounds stripped, built more like a footballer than a scholar and still handsome in a rugged way, despite the bald spot and the greying temples, this active rake with the brooding features, full lips and hard blue eyes certainly went from woman to woman, but his motives were not those generally assumed by other men. It was ironical that Morrell should provide them with a focus for their more reactionary fantasies in the matter of sex. Morrell was not indulging in lechery; he was seeking, above all, a maternal solicitude.

Each new liaison was no mere adventure for him, it was the occasion of a unique hope. Though the hope might fail again and again, Morrell could not settle for permanent disappointment. The same stubborn and resourceful streak in his nature that led him to battle on with his researches in face of frequent disappointments showed itself in his relations with women. The failure of any single experiment did not mean that there would *never* be a success. Following this axiom, the reputation of the scientist mounted; the tally of the amorist lengthened; but the sense of having missed out was never finally laid to rest.

His male colleagues might smile at his escapades, but Edna, his wife, did not find them so amusing. He regretted that, but could do nothing about it. There had been a time when he had flinched from looking too closely at his wife's face, not wishing to see the bleakness that had settled on it. Edna when they first married had been a gentle girl, fluffy-haired, with dove-grey eyes. He had found her very pretty, but her devotion had seemed the more important thing. That had long since ceased to be available. When her husband was driven to look elsewhere, Edna's face and heart had set hard. For a while she had stalked through Morrell's life, confronting him at every moment with haughty reproach, but now she had become resigned and turned, with middle age, to religion.

Morrell was sad to have inflicted so much grief on his wife, but this was an old failure and there had been others since. When his thoughts turned to Edna he still knew regret but the feeling was dulled by time and habit. He could at least claim that he had always done his best to look after her. He remained considerate, knowing all too well the pains of loss, but his hope had long since moved elsewhere. At this time, his hope and his love were centred on Judith Glass, a dark, vivacious girl only a few years older than his daughter, Sandra. Judith was generous, offering her young body to him without reservation, but, more important, she was intuitive and sympathetic, not abashed when he laid his greying head between her breasts, able to comfort the child in him.

Judith was special to Morrell in every way. Not only did she offer him love, she could share his interests and offer him encouragement. She was herself a trained biologist and he had first met her when she joined the staff of his research establishment. That had been a year ago. When he had hesitated about making the trip to England, it was Judith who persuaded him to go. She understood how much part of him longed for this sort of honour. When he had told the Government about the possibility of such a trip, no less a person than Senator Thorwaldson, a member of the National Security Council, had pressed him to make the visit a brief one, time being of the essence, as the Senator put it. But it was not Thorwaldson so much as Judith who would draw him back to his Spring Harbour laboratory as soon as possible. He thought of her dark lustrous eyes, the quirky, mischievous mouth, and he smiled as he walked among the crowds of Oxford Street. Then he remembered the man, Garen, dodging about somewhere behind him and his smile faded. He was being watched – and that was like the end of innocent. The presence of Garen, the agent, did not suggest danger to Morrell. Garen appeared to him instead as the embodiment of a fallen world. Professor Morrell did not like to think of Garen shadowing his progress through these sunlit streets. Indeed, when Ambassador Brock had informed Morrell that he would be kept under light surveillance during the two days of his stay in England, Morrell had been indignant. He had made his protest, but Brock, in his suave way, had been immovable. Instructions had come down from the highest level, and that was that.

'It's a thing that has never been necessary before,' Morrell complained, 'and I'm sure it isn't now.'

'You have never been quite so important before,' said the

Ambassador, smiling, seeking to touch the nerve of vanity in the man. 'We don't envisage any . . . problems,' he added. 'And the officer will be discreet.'

'I would rather not be followed, all the same,' Morrell retorted. The brightness of the ceremony at Oxford seemed tarnished by the idea. He felt uneasy, brought up sharp against the ambiguities of his moral position. Ethics demanded one thing of him, patriotism another. Somebody had once written that patriotism was the last refuge of the scoundrel. Who was it? He could not remember. And yet, he argued, to refuse co-operation, to reject the appeals of his own government after everything had been explained to him – that would have been even more unthinkable.

'As to being important,' said Morrell, '*there* is the measure of my importance!' He pointed to a brief paragraph at the foot of a column in that morning's *Times*. It reported the arrival of Professor A. Morrell, noted micro-biologist, whose recent work had led to new understanding of the mechanisms of cell replication, and in the longer term might well have a bearing on the control of cancer. It went on to give a brief itinerary of his visit, stating Professor Morrell would that day be the guest of the American Ambassador and next morning would travel up to Oxford to receive his honorary degree. He would then address a meeting of his fellow-scientists and attend a dinner given in his honour before leaving Oxford to catch a night plane to New York.

'A very modest degree of fame, don't you think?' asked Morrell.

The Ambassador smiled again. This tantrum on the part of the scientist bored him, but he gave no sign of his feelings. He could feel scant sympathy with the fellow, but he was prepared to humour him. The Ambassador urged Morrell to regard surveillance as an indication of the value placed on him by the Government of the United States.

Ambassador Brock had not been told the precise nature of Morrell's importance, from which he concluded that it must be considerable, and of a sensitive nature, but his instructions had been quite clear. He was to arrange that the Professor be given an escort for the duration of his visit. The directive also stressed that this should be done discreetly, not in the Ambassador's judgement because of any resistance Morrell might show towards the idea, but because the Government did not wish to advertise their interest in the man to the eyes of others. Ambassador Brock set about the task of persuading this touchy academic to go along with the decision of Government. By the end of twenty minutes, he had brought Morrell to the point of agreement. It had been a wearisome little exercise in diplomacy for the Ambassador. 'Good,' he said. 'That's understood, then.' The smile was nailed to his face. 'One of our men will be keeping a friendly eye on you from now on.'

'Yes,' said Morrel stiffly. 'If he must.'

'And tomorrow, when the car is placed at your disposal for the trip to Oxford, the same man will act as your chauffeur. I take it there's no objection?'

Morrell gave a resigned nod.

'Well, then, I think you two had better make each other's acquaintance,' said the Ambassador. 'Mr Garen is assigned to look after you. A reliable officer, so I'm led to believe. I don't deal with such matters directly, you understand. They fall within the province of Mr Vogel.'

Grudgingly, Morrell allowed himself to be introduced, first to Vogel and then to Walter Garen, the balding agent who was to act as his bodyguard. He took the agent's blunt hand in his and looked into a face whose coarse features seemed somehow smudged. All but the eyes. They were sharp enough, but their sharpness spoke to Morrell of a soiled, devious world.

Morrell knew that Garen must be somewhere not far behind him among the crowds of Oxford Street but he was unaware that another man was following the same route as himself and the agent. This man was about thirty years old, tall and broad-shouldered. His skin was deeply tanned and his hair bleached by years of exposure to a hot sun. He wore a blue sweater and faded jeans and he carried over his shoulder a bag stamped with the words *Qantas Airlines*. He looked like a tourist who had spent the summer somewhere on the shores of the Mediterranean and had now come late in the year to take a look round London.

The tourist seemed to share Professor Morrell's interest in the works of art displayed by the Bond Street galleries. Later, when Morrell turned down Charing Cross Road, intent on finding a book he had seen favourably reviewed in the latest edition of *Nature*, the tourist followed in the same direction, though still at some distance from Morrell. Chance appeared to lead them both into the same bookshop, though the tourist stayed there only a moment. Apparently the section on archaeology did not have what he was seeking. He stood, hesitating, as if doubtful whether to approach the assistant. Then he gave a shrug, adjusted his *Qantas* bag, and left the shop.

The Professor went on to keep the appointment he had made with his old friend and colleague, Doctor Haltrecht, and the tourist took a bus to Notting Hill Gate. Once there, he entered a flat in one of the rows of houses off Campden Hill Road, where he joined a slender moustachioed man, dressed like a young executive, and a pretty girl whose hair was no longer blonde. They seemed glad to see him.

2

The three young people sat down together at a table in the middle of the room. Each laid a number of photographs on the table, rather as if they were playing some eccentric card-game. Professor Morrell figured prominently in all the photographs, but he did not seem to be the major source of interest to them just then. The tourist picked up a felt-tip pen and drew a circle round another face, a blunt smudged undistinguished

15

face which appeared regularly in the background of the snap-shots they had gathered that day.

'There,' he said. 'That one. He's always on parade. Take a good look, David, Rachel. You see. There's just him. Just the one.'

Rachel frowned at the picture of Garen. The grossness of the man's face troubled her. His eyes were hard, narrowed to slits. 'Couldn't there be others, Moishe?' she asked timorously.

'No,' said the big man. 'I think not. They're using light cover. That makes sense. I'd do the same in their place.'

'Then you'd be wrong, too,' David laughed and ran a nervous finger along the curve of his moustache. He took a cutting from his pocket. It was the brief account in that morning's *Times*, reporting Professor Morrell's arrival. He put it down on the table and smoothed out the creases.

'This confirms things,' he said.

'Could it be better?' asked Moishe, after reading the report. His English was fluent, but there was a slight thickness about it, a guttural inflection. He tapped the slip of paper. 'It's on, children!' he said to the others. 'Just as they leave Oxford. Pouf! Gone like a puff of smoke and not a soul the wiser. Nobody will know. Nobody *must* know. Not till we choose to give them the news.'

The others nodded. They had been through this before. They had rehearsed it many times. All the same, secrecy was essential, the cornerstone of their plan, and therefore the point could bear a great deal of repetition.

'The terms are there?'

'Definitely. Box 458,' said David in a tight voice.

Moishe nodded.

Rachel sought out David's eyes, trying to see how he felt. For her own part, she could hardly believe it. The planning had been like a game, the desperate audacity of the scheme they had devised like a fantasy of revenge, such as children make up to punish their giant tormentors of the adult world. Now it was to happen. And soon. The realization pierced her sharply enough to make her hunch forward. She saw the fervent gleam in David's eyes and understood his exaltation and his fear. He was worried about how he would acquit himself : his life so far had scarcely been that of a man of action. Moishe looked calm, but then, Moishe had experience of such matters – violence, betrayal, intrigue, sudden death. She and David relied on Moishe to guide them in this new dangerous world. Moishe was calm, as usual, but she felt it was a bitter calm, a terrible calm.

Moishe has been through too much, she thought. He had once admitted it to them. 'I am spoilt for ordinary life,' he had told them. 'No good at it. I've tried but it's no use. I can't settle. There's not enough quietness left in my head.' Moishe had been drunk when he made that admission. Sober, he would not discuss his state of mind, though sometimes he would talk about things he had seen, actions he had taken part in. He always spoke casually, without emphasis, so that at first it seemed he did not realize the enormity of what he was saying, as if the nerve of imagination had been killed in him, leaving only a coarse indifference, like that of a mercenary. But as you listened, you came to understand the grief pent up in Moishe's heart. There was a bitter, crazy man locked up in there. The casual manner and the wry jokes were guards he set over this devil howling for retribution.

'A free night, *chaverim*,' said Moishe. 'How will you spend it?'

'I don't know.' David tried to strike the same cool note. He smiled, grateful for the word *chaverim*. 'Comrades', he thought, spoken in the holy tongue, like a bond between them, the language itself a reminder of their high purpose. David's eyes grew moist. He had to blink away tears.

'Relax, cousin. Why not take Rachel to the movies? A restaurant? Make the most of the evening.'

Moishe left the rest unspoken but they all knew : this might be the last opportunity. If things went badly, this could be their last day of freedom, maybe even their last day on earth. It did not seem to David like a time for movies. He thought of the man in the photographs, the man whose face Moishe

17

had ringed with the felt pen. It was a lacklustre face, not obviously blessed by any gifts of character or intelligence. Dull and hard-favoured, it was the sort of countenance you could easily imagine sitting on the shoulders of an executioner.

David swallowed with some difficulty, aware that Moishe was watching him. He wanted to say to Moishe: 'I am not afraid, cousin, not exactly afraid, but I'm not used to these situations. You will have to make some allowances for a beginner.' He did not trust himself to speak. He knew Moishe thought he gave way too easily to emotion. Once, in a moment of irritation, Moishe had called him a 'ghetto Jew'. It had certainly not been intended as a compliment, though Moishe had managed to smile whilst he said it. 'And am I to be ashamed of that?' David had responded hotly. 'You want me to be ashamed of our past? Ashamed of my race?'

Moishe did not answer at first, just stared at him with those faded blue eyes. Finally he said, 'No, of course. You must forgive me, David.'

All the same, Moishe had sounded discouraged and David understood why. He knew Moishe was troubled by the Jewish past, repelled by all that fell under the term *yiddishkeit*, afraid of the subtle, intricate heritage of the ghetto, its influence on the soul of the people. Moishe felt that at this moment in history the Jew must be the *Sabra*. He must be the thorny fruit of the desert cactus, the man of action: tough, practical, in charge of his fate. In the name of survival, Moishe was willing to deny all those huddled, passionate, ecstatic generations, the very thought of whom made David's eyes fill with tears; deny them, and even deny the Holy Name itself. Moishe rejected the faith of his fathers, the covenant at Sinai, the laws of Moses; and spoke bitterly of the systematic delusions which had been fastened like shackles upon his race. Moishe saw in them the way of weakness which had led to the infinite woes of Auschwitz, and he was afraid that this trait might yet betray the people again, delivering them into a new bondage.

David understood Moishe's position but he did not accept it. One way or another, the ghetto had been the world of the

Jews for more than a thousand years. It had been their *only* world until the day before yesterday. If all that the ghetto stubbornly cherished were now to be rooted out of the Jewish heritage, how much of value would remain? How much survive of the authentic substance of the House of Abraham? With so much discarded, would the inhabitants of Israel be any more than the nationals of a small Levantine state, noted for ferocity more than understanding, technology rather than true learning? David's answer was different from that of Moishe. He did not choose to discard but to embrace. Born the son of an unobservant household, he had gone back deliberately to the hopes and beliefs of the past. He had become a pious Orthodox Jew – much to the amazement of his father, the Brighton antique dealer.

Now Moishe smiled at David and then at Rachel. 'The movies?' he repeated. 'Why not the movies?'

David shook his head. 'I don't think so.'

'Ah, well. This is the worst time, children. Always. Just before things start.' Moishe got up and put on his coat.

'You're going out?' asked Rachel. She wanted Moishe to leave them alone for a while and yet she felt unsettled by the idea of his absence.

'A couple of things I have to check,' said Moishe. 'At the house.' And he left them.

David and Rachel were glad to be alone. There was a lot they meant to say on this night and yet, now they were here, it was hard to find the right words. They sat together on the sofa, watching the light fade out of the sky, speaking very little. Tomorrow hung over them like a cliff. They sat holding hands while the house-roofs opposite turned black as jet.

'Afterwards . . .' said David.

'Afterwards we shall go back. Shan't we?'

'Yes. Oh yes, we shall go back.'

'Jacob's Hill,' said Rachel. The memory of their summer there was very poignant now. She had a vision of peace, strenuous peace among the hills of Galilee, though properly

19

speaking there had been no peace. The kibbutz was near the border. People carried guns into the fields.

'And we'll be married there, Rachel. In the faith.'

'Under the *chuppah*,' she whispered, squeezing his hand.

Silence fell once more. They leant together, finding comfort in each other's bodies.

'By this time tomorrow . . .' murmured Rachel, awe in her voice.

'I know. I was thinking the same. It will be over, Rachel.'

'The first part will be over.'

The dusk lay softly, a tender light. Their voices sounded wistful, like lovers at a parting. Both were very much aware of the guns lying in the cupboard, waiting, just as they were waiting. They had got used to having weapons in the flat, but now the guns had grown important and demanding again.

'It's not easy,' said Rachel. 'I don't find it easy to come to terms with, David.'

He knew what she meant but he would not speak, would not acknowledge the difficulty.

'I mean . . . using force,' she persisted.

'*You* can say that, Rachel? You, a student of history!' David gave a wild exaggerated laugh.

'For *us*,' urged Rachel. 'Oh, I know about the others. All the ruthless people. I can imagine that. But *us*?'

'It's a trick we have to learn.'

They were motionless, unsure, a little daunted by the demands they foresaw being made on them. They were strangers to heroism.

'There needn't be any bloodshed,' said David. 'I'm sure there won't be. Everything will work, Rachel. You'll see.'

'Moishe?' said Rachel timidly. 'He is one of the ruthless people?'

'And if he is,' said David fiercely, 'he has had good cause. Moishe is right,' he added. 'We are being sold out, Rachel. Bit by bit. Do they think we're all blind?'

'I know,' breathed Rachel, clutching at his arm. 'Oh, I know. I believe it, too.'

'Betrayed!' exclaimed David. The harsh word fed his anger, making him feel strong and righteous again. 'Deserted. By stealth. We let that happen? We stand by meekly and allow it? No, no. Somebody has to act.'

'David . . . what if they don't agree?'

There was a moment's hesitation and then David said, 'It won't come to that. They have no choice.'

'Ah,' murmured Rachel. She did not press the point. She shut her mind against the murderous alternative.

'You don't have to come, you know.' David lit a cigarette. 'It would be all right.'

'Oh no, David!'

'Moishe and I could manage the thing.' He gestured to show his confidence and the tip of the cigarette traced a glowing arc in the dusk.

'But I *want* to be with you, David. I want to be part of it. I love you.' To Rachel, the thrust of this argument was beyond dispute.

'You are already part of it. You put up the money. We had to have that.'

'Oh, the money. The money. That isn't really mine. It just came down to me. Aunt Hannah died, that's all. It's old de Sousa money. I don't count that.'

'All the same . . .' said David in the voice of an indigent research student. Money counted to him. It was different for Rachel; she had been born into a rich Sephardic family and had never known the lack of money. She was blessed with an indulgent father, a merchant banker, an elegant moth of a man with silver hair. It was strange: Abram de Sousa contributed generously to the National Fund but he had never quite managed to find the time to go to Israel – and this though he went on repeating the pious hope, 'Next year in Jerusalem', at each Passover meal. Who could guess what the words meant to such a man now? David found it hard to imagine. On the other hand, he could guess pretty well what Mr de Sousa's response would be should he find that his daughter was being led into such a desperate venture as the one they would be embarking on tomorrow. Mr de Sousa would be appalled. His was still a respectable, gentlemanly world.

Rachel thrust her face towards him. 'You think I'm too scared,' she said hotly. 'Isn't that it?'

'I don't know about you being scared,' said David with a laugh. 'I'm damned sure I am.' He was glad to find a context in which he could admit his fear.

She threw her arms round him. 'Darling David! We'll do it together. All three of us. Moishe agreed that would be best. He said a woman was a good idea, remember? He said a woman could come in useful on a job.'

'He said a tough woman,' said David gently. 'A ruthless woman. Is that you?'

Rachel snatched the cigarette from between his fingers and pressed the burning tip of it against her forearm.

'What the hell are you doing?' David knocked the cigarette out of her hand and stamped furiously on it.

'You see!' cried Rachel, struggling to keep her voice steady against the pain.

David leant his head against her shoulder. She could feel him trembling. 'All right,' he whispered. 'All right.'

'I'm coming with you, David?'

'Yes,' he said. 'You're coming,' his voice troubled, his nostrils flaring at the odour of singed flesh.

David covered his head with a black skull-cap and offered up his evening prayer to the God of his fathers. Rachel shared the moment, her dark hair hidden again by the blonde wig she had worn earlier that day when she stood outside the American Embassy. Now the wig did duty as a *sheital*. Rachel had been brought up in an observant house, and though not particularly devout before, she was happy to go along with David's new fervour, saw nothing odd in it, but regarded it as a likely enough destination for a Jewish man to reach. When Rachel first met David at Oxford, he had been very much the scientific agnostic, a micro-biologist, scornful of all religions, ready to discount what he called 'the accident of race', and apt to suggest that her somewhat wavering compliance with the dietary laws cast grave doubt on her intelligence. She had let him have his say, but he had never been able to convince her that the manner of life in which she had been brought up should be abandoned for anything so arid as a point of intellectual principle. She had kept a stubborn, silent hold on her beliefs; to deny them would have struck at so much : at her family, her memories of the past, the happy times of her childhood, Chanukah, Purim. She clung womanlike to all that, meanwhile humouring her prickly young lover, and in the end, David had swung round completely, as she had always felt he might. Now, by the fairly relaxed standards of her own family, he had become astoundingly devout. But this was a matter of pride, tinged only faintly with concern. Hearing him intone the *Shema,* she was very much happier than she had ever been hearing him dismiss all such prayers as empty formulae. Indeed, she was tempted to regard David's change of mind as a confirmation of her instinctive belief that prayers could sometimes be answered, that God *was* good and cared for his creation, that there was love and meaning in the world, dignity for all mankind, and a special destiny for God's chosen people.

David's commitment to religion was much more fierce than Rachel's because it was that much less secure. His beliefs did not spring spontaneously out of the fabric of his life, as Rachel's did; they were the result of a conscious choice made to bring to an end a time of spiritual confusion. Others might think him unassailably convinced, but David knew his demonstrations of piety were, in part at least, a rebuke to the doubts that lingered in his heart. He was not naturally of a religious temperament and he had been brought up in a household that did not concern itself with worship. His parents were the sort of people who were interested in prosperity and social acceptance. In pursuit of this ambition they had merged almost completely with the Gentile majority. In view of their preferences, it was an ironical misfortune that both

Mr Schuster and his wife, Leah, possessed features that were unmistakably Jewish, though Leah had done her best to repair this bad casting on the part of the Creator with the help of a plastic surgeon. She now looked like a Jewess who has had her nose straightened.

David's parents saw little of him now. He declined to eat any longer at their table, saying their food was *trefe*, and had relapsed into all the old superstitions the Schusters hoped they had left behind for ever. Sometimes Leah enquired of her husband how they could ever have got such a son but Mr Schuster was not much help when it came to unravelling the mysteries of heredity. His response was either to reach for his golf clubs or to turn the television up.

David prayed on in the face of his own uncertainties. It was more than a year now since he had made the decision. He had chosen to take back on to himself the entire obligation of his people to God and history, not only those parts that were easy or fashionable, nor those that did not clash too uncomfortably with the dictates of reason, but all of it. For a man of his kind, half measures had seemed worse than nothing.

'Blessed are you,' he prayed, 'O Lord our God, the God of our fathers, God of Abraham, God of Isaac and God of Jacob. God who is great, strong and awesome, the most high God who bestows goodness, who owns all things, who remembers the goodness of the fathers and will bring a redeemer to their children's children.'

He felt the power of the ancient words and longed to believe absolutely in their truth. He would certainly act as if they were true. There were troubling aspects of his return to Judaism. He was uneasily aware that in rescuing his God, he had also been rescuing himself. When he affirmed the Holy One, he was also endorsing his own identity. A year ago he had looked at himself and found a man with neither race nor country, a mongrel, clever but purposeless, thrown into despair by the empty universe which was all that science had offered him in the end. Judaism had healed him of that despair, given him back an ancient lineage, restored purpose to his life. And

24

yet, did the God of Abraham really exist? And the Covenant struck at Sinai? Part of him would never be able to set aside his doubts.

'You are hallowed,' he proclaimed stubbornly, 'and your name is hallowed. Holy ones praise you each day. Selah.'

Yet once the first great leap into belief was taken, the world had revealed an inner logic. David became not only a religious man but a man who, like the God he praised, must keep faith with those who slept in the dust. A Zionist of the Zionists, a zealot spurning compromise.

'Sound the great horn of our freedom,' he urged his Maker. 'Raise your banner to draw in the exiles. Gather us from the four corners of the world.'

As David spoke these words, his doubts vanished. He was rewarded with a pure uprush of joy, remembering how they had knelt to kiss the soil of the land, he and Rachel together, when they made their own return for a few weeks last summer. Soon they would go back again and this time it would be for ever. Yet first there was this task to accomplish, this awesome duty, the need for which had been made clear to them, not by chance, so he believed, but by the workings of the Divine Will. He knew there could be no personal salvation for a Jew if the general deliverance were allowed to fail. *Eretz Yisrael* must be secured.

'To slanderers let there be no hope,' he prayed, bitterness on his tongue, thinking of those allies who were even now busy with their policies of covert betrayal, those powerful 'friends' among the nations of this world whose minds were being swayed by new expediencies. They were asking each other in their secret councils: 'How much is Israel worth to us? How far can we agree to the dismantling of the state? Remember, we must not lose face!'

'May the enemies of all your people swiftly be cut off,' said David, speaking through clenched teeth, so that the words came out more as a threat than a plea. 'May the men of violence be rooted out, smashed, thrown down and humbled. Soon. In our time.'

David's voice swelled triumphantly.

'. . . And to Jerusalem your city, return in mercy, and dwell there as you have promised, and build it soon . . . in our time.'

Exaltation made him tremble: 'Accept, O Lord, your people, Israel . . . receive with favour their offerings and prayers . . . and may our eyes see you return to Zion in mercy.' The litanies swept him along to their conclusion: 'Blessed are you, O Lord, who will bless your people Israel with peace. With peace.'

David and Rachel stood silent in the near-dark. They felt the words of the Service as more than an affirmation of their faith. They had been dedicating themselves to what lay ahead tomorrow.

In a little while David reached out and took Rachel's hand. She turned towards him. When her caressing fingers touched his face, he did not try to hide from her that his cheeks were wet. She understood his tears. It was from Moishe that tears must be hidden.

3

Moishe drove the grey Rover across north-west London, making his way to a district that lay on the fringes of the city, an area where rows of houses straggled among forlorn vestiges of countryside. His destination was Mount Vernon Road, an address that had once hoped to be rather grand. The houses along the road were Edwardian villas with bay windows and steep gables; detached residences set in their own gardens, the biggest of them almost hidden behind walls and trees. The houses had been meant for people who were going up in the world, but time and fashion had pronounced against them and now, with their flaking paint and neglected gardens, their rusty ironwork and shabby porches, they looked what they were : the wrecks of a genteel dream.

In one or two of the houses, old ladies still lingered out of the earlier time, making their slow circuits of a world of brass and heavy mahogany, populating the emptiness with cats, but most of the houses had long since been split up into apartments which were neither choice nor convenient and were lived in by a shifting population who only stayed there until they could find something better. These lodgers felt no allegiance for Mount Vernon Road and showed little curiosity about what went on there. This fact, together with the general location of the place, was what had led Moishe to choose a house there.

Moishe drew the car to a halt beside a tall wooden gate. It had been built from stout timbers, and a long time ago somebody had painted it green. Although two of the planks were rotten now, the top of the gate still displayed a row of iron spikes. Similarly, the high wall round the garden was still studded along its top with shards and knuckles of green bottle-glass, at least where the coping had not cracked and slipped away. These dilapidated bourgeois defences gave the place a forbidding look, but they were a welcome sight to Moishe, as were the dense overgrown shrubberies on the far side of the wall, which ensured that the house was hidden from the road. Only the pinnacle of a foolish turret rose above sombre thickets of holly and laurel.

Moishe smiled as he pushed open the gate. According to David and Rachel, the house-agent had been scarcely able to restrain his emotion at the prospect of a sale. The property must have lain on his books for God knows how long. In the grip of his astonishment, all that the house-agent had been able to muster was the doubtful assurance that so *much* could be done with a house of this sort! It had been left partly furnished, and of course, if any of the furniture should prove to be of use . . .

Well, so much *had* been done, thought Moishe wryly, taking the Rover up the drive. Would the house-agent have approved their efforts so far? He would surely have been impressed by the way they had taken the garden in hand. Moishe himself had cut down all weeds and scrub within a thirty-yard radius of the house, which made the place look a lot tidier and had the added advantage of allowing them an unobstructed field of fire. There had been progress on the inside, too. The house had received a modest amount of new furniture, including a deal table, a cardboard box full of pans and crockery, three mattresses, an Ingram sub-machine gun with folding stock, and a couple of 7·62 mm. SLR rifles fitted with telescopic sights. They had not bothered to get rid of the old armchairs and mildewed cupboards already in the house. As well let them stay. Mains services were now connected and the house was ready for immediate occupation. Nor had the security of the householder been overlooked, thought Moishe, still pursuing his joke. Bars had been fitted to the windows, and all exterior doors, save the front one by which Moishe was now entering the building, had been locked, bolted and battened down with heavy lengths of wood. It was a place where a man might hope to rest easy, even in today's troubled times!

Moishe had not arrived empty-handed. He was carrying a couple of five-gallon plastic buckets and in his pocket there was a box of white candles. It was true, thought Moishe, that mains services were connected, but you never knew – there might just be a discontinuity of supply. The buckets and the candles were a precaution against bad luck. Moishe did not expect them to be used. Nevertheless, he put the candles away safely in a drawer, he filled the buckets with water and placed them in a corner of the living-room, and then went on in the same spirit to take the rifles from their cupboard and check them. Everything was as it should be. The new owners could move in tomorrow – and they would start entertaining right away!

So far Moishe had managed to conduct himself with a kind of dry levity. He knew this was his best recourse, but he did not expect to be able to keep it up much longer. There was another mood growing in him. He had felt it from the moment he took the rifles in his hands. Moishe was no stranger to guns. In fact, he knew them very well, familiar accomplices from the days of his youth, though unlike him they had never lost their assurance. Guns remained themselves, as sleek and elegant as ever, the imperturbable dandies of murder. Whereas he kept changing. Sometimes nowadays he grew sullen with despair or gave way to an almost manic hilarity. He was no longer dependable. That, of course, was why the Bureau in Tel Aviv had retired him. They had not told him, not in so many words. Instead they talked about his age, a man turned thirty who had seen so much hard service. They meant he was no longer entirely stable, no longer quite trustworthy, but then, thought Moishe, a man who has spent the greater part of a decade performing acts of violence in their service could be expected to show some small measure of instability.

It was only then that Moishe had come to recognize another virtue of guns. It was this: guns kept faith. They remained available. They had no favourites. They would still come to the hand of the desperate and the outcast. They were the final remedy against injustice and betrayal. Without them, your voice could never hope to reach those lofty Chancelleries and Departments of State where politicians supplemented their public pledges with private threats, and edged a nation towards disaster to further their own convenience. How high did the cost of a gallon of petrol have to rise, thought Moishe bitterly, before it became cheaper to connive at the ruin of a state? Moishe felt the question grind down on him.

It was not only the killings that had led Moishe into desolation, not only the shit and stench and the corpses among the rocks, the houses blown up while women wept, the murderous counter-stroke at Gaza, the bloody border raiding, the assassination of a terrorist leader he had personally arranged in Beirut, whose dead face had looked uncannily like that of his own father, it was not only these things in themselves, it was the realization that all this might have been for nothing. Moishe had watched with growing consternation while the Jewish state was forced to bow to hidden pressures.

The feeling had started at that moment in the war of '73 when the enemy was let out of the iron noose and Israeli armour ground sullenly back across the Canal bridges. Moishe had watched the evidence accumulate: pledges accepted from those who in the past had never kept their word; victorious armies ordered to give up lands bought with their blood; the handing back of the Abu Rodeis oilfields; the withdrawal behind the Sinai passes; the glib talk of an independent Arab state of the West Bank. Behind it all, Moishe was convinced, there lay the hidden pressure exerted by powerful nations on his country's government. Moishe understood that the destruction of Israel had become only a matter of time and opportunity. When he arrived at this conclusion, Moishe had joined his voice with those of the so-called extremists, men from such parties as the *Gush Enunim*, who would not willingly relinquish a foot of ground – which was another reason why the Bureau had let him go. He had become untrustworthy in more ways than one: he had remained a hawk when hawks were out of favour.

Moishe sat down in one of the armchairs. He knew the signs. He was about to live again through the events that began with him seeing the cat. They often came back to him before the start of a new operation. With a sigh, he surrendered himself to them again.

The cat, he thought, the cat is lying on a warm slab of concrete, basking in the sun. It washes itself lazily, a black cat with yellow eyes. Some fifty yards away stands the schoolhouse, a white building, very plain in design, its walls glaring in the sunlight except where the dark dangerous windows cut into the façade. No sound comes from the schoolhouse, though there are thirty children trapped in there.

Moishe is crouching with the commandos behind a low stone wall, the sun warm on his back. He waits, balancing a Sterling in his hand, watching the cat flick its ears at a fly. Then the cat yawns, displaying a delicate coral arch behind the sharp teeth.

There are four of the bastards in there, four terrorists shut up with the kids. They slipped over the border last night, skulked in a hut until morning and then gunned down the first two people who happened to come their way. After that, they ran into the school and took it over. The children had just started lessons. They are still there. The children will be lying on the floor now. That kind of training comes into the curriculum very early, up here in the frontier settlements.

The gunmen will be on their feet, staring out of those dark windows. They have already tried to make a bargain. One of them has called out in Hebrew: 'Let us go. We will take the children but we swear we will release them once we are over the border.' It is not good enough. You cannot trust these people to keep their word. Besides, there are the demands of policy to consider. Even at moments as bad as these, the general directive still stands: No deals: No weakness. These men have killed twice already. They cannot be allowed to escape with their lives. Moishe tries not to think of the children shut up behind the white walls.

The commando officer has been urging the terrorists to let the children go, but they are not likely to do that. The officer's voice lacks conviction. Even as he speaks, he knows it will not happen. The children are still going to be there when the place is stormed. It has to be done fast, a rush from all sides. Just the same, thinks Moishe, how long does it take a man to swing his automatic weapon in a last act of malice? Will the terrorists allow themselves such a monstrous indulgence in the final few seconds before the commandos overrun them? Or will humanity triumph over hatred? Perhaps, but it is not a good bet. Moishe is troubled by their numbers. Four is too many. It only takes one crazy man.

There are a couple of minutes left before the assault is due to start. Moishe watches the cat settle into sleep.

Once the action begins, it is all over very quickly. Moishe experiences it as a moment of mad, grunting abandonment in which the earth seems to tilt and sway. The gunfire is very loud; there is a whistle blowing; glass shatters; woodwork tears and splinters; men fall down.

By the time Moishe gets into the schoolroom, the terrorists are all dead. So are seven of the children. The other kids huddle against the walls, dazed. This is a very bad time for Moishe, one of the worst times of all, as bad as when he heard of the death of his brother Simon, ambushed on the Metulla road. He is filled with such rage at the sight of the dead children that he wants to commit some sort of outrage on the nearest terrorist, stamp his boot into the lifeless face, rip up the corpse with bullets. They could have let the kids go, he thinks bitterly, but at least he knows the terrorists did not deliberately set out to slaughter them. They could have done that, perhaps they felt the temptation, but they had managed to do without that kind of revenge. Moishe knows that the children have been killed by accident and that the bullets which hit them might well have come from the guns of the commandos. From his own gun? A profound sadness settles on Moishe. He stares down at the nearest terrorist, the one whose face only a moment before he had been eager to grind under his heel. It is a very young face. The moustache is still wispy thought the brows are firmly drawn and the eyelashes long. It could easily be the face of a Jewish boy if it were not for the headgear. Moishe sees that all the terrorists have chosen to don the *keffiyeh* as they waited for death. He can imagine the scene, these four young men putting on the checkered headcloth and crowning it with the coiled *agál*, their sombre robing performed under the wide eyes of enemy children. They will have urged each other to look on death bravely, thinks Moishe. Each side has its honour, and they have done well enough in their fashion. They killed two men in cold blood but at least they resisted the temptation to turn their guns on children.

Looking from the dead terrorists to the dead children, Moishe becomes aware of a grief in himself that is no longer simple. He thinks of leaders, old influential men who sit in offices arranging the statistics of death. For them, these are matters of policy. He sees there are many kinds of victims.

He is aware of the calculations, the subterfuges, the bloody arithmetic of power at which those old politicals are so adept. Beside them the gunmen are naïve idealists, mere innocents, deliberately sacrificed.

Since that moment Moishe has felt uneasy at the idea of authority, whatever its source. He has been troubled by a sense of the innate criminality of power.

With this thought firmly in his mind, Moishe began to consider the action that would begin tomorrow.

As for the memory, it ended as it always did. When Moishe went outside the schoolhouse, away from the carnage, he saw the cat again. It had not moved. There it lay on the concrete flagstone, still sleeping in the sun. Nearby sprawled the body of a fallen commando, and they were just carrying one of the dead children away.

Moishe drove back across London, very alive to the buzz and stir of the city by night, the myriad lives being lived, the innumerable swarm of hopes and fears. His senses heightened by expectation, Moishe was moved by the thought of all the people out there, trapped in the various webs that were spun for them, struggling to survive as far as tomorrow. God, how many different kinds of victims existed in the world! Well, his own tomorrow would be different. The three of them had found a way to shake the arrogant assumptions of the rulers of the world – and in particular of that damned juggler, that ace politician, hopping from capital to capital, pulling treaties out of his hat. He was about to learn that he was not invulnerable.

4

Walter Garen inspected himself at the wardrobe mirror. He did not mind the blue serge suit too much, but the peaked cap depressed him. He looked like a bit player in an old movie. A nobody. Just the guy who opened the door. Garen could see no need for the cap, but Vogel had insisted on the whole goddam outfit. Maybe Vogel thought it was funny to see him wearing the cap.

He shrugged. What did it matter? This was a bum assignment. He got no other kind nowadays and knew he could expect none. He was lucky still to be in the Service. As an agent he was blown, finished, the other side had got his number long ago, and besides, he was growing old for the business. No, that wasn't true. He was still a hard man. The body was in good trim. He regarded his smudgy features without affection. They had always seemed like a slander on him. He was no dumb ox. Maybe no genius either, but he had his quota of brains. He had done all right in the 'Fifties. They had played it straight down the line in those days. Now half the guys in the Service looked like freaks. Take Vogel. Garen stirred uneasily. His feelings about Vogel were mixed. Vogel was his superior and as such had an automatic right to his respect. OK, he gave the man his respect, but the fact of the matter was that Vogel was fifteen years his junior, and the guy had hair down to his shoulders. He might be fronting as a cultural attaché, but did that mean he had to walk around looking like a fag? He told himself Vogel had been lucky in his area of operation. That explained a lot. Things had gone pretty good for the guys in the African theatre. Garen held up his left hand and looked at it. The index finger was no more than a stump. He had lost that in action. Six years wasted.

34

It was not his failure. He had not been the one to louse up the Vietnam operation. He had come out the far side of that tunnel, like many another good man, with nothing to show for it but wound-scars and grey hairs. He stared at the stump morosely and speculated on the only place Vogel was likely to lose a finger. But it was no use thinking like that. He knew he was dependent on Vogel now. One adverse report and he'd be finished. He was simply wearing out his time here. The future yawned, dark and null. Where would he go? Probably end up where he'd begun, in some place like that crummy Detroit apartment he'd done his growing up in. Wherever it was, he would be alone. He did not have a wife. In the Service, commitments such as that could hold you back.

Garen had taken what seemed to him to be the safe way and now was left with confused memories of American broads, lank-haired fräuleins, slant-eyed Vietnamese dolls, all of them either his hired accomplices or his victims. Love had always been too dangerous a demand to make. Those women, he thought, those bints, they must be used up by now. He felt a movement of regret, sour as a belch.

Now Garen no longer wanted women very much, he would secretly have liked to marry one. But he had no illusions on that score : it was too late. He sighed. The world was a rough place and sometimes Garen felt he had not been dealt a full hand.

Garen touched the gun in his shoulder-holster. He was good for a while yet. He wished he could prove it to Vogel but did not think he would get the chance. This job was a long way down the field from being hit man in Berlin. Hell, thought Garen, it gave a guy no chance to shine! He shrugged his big shoulders and went off to the briefing.

John Vogel looked at the sullen grudging face on the other side of the desk. As always, Garen's knobbly features suggested to him an unfinished piece of work, a clay model that the sculptor had roughed out and then abandoned as a flop. He gathered that Garen was still touchy about the assignment,

35

and he guessed that the older man regarded the task as demeaning. Not that Garen would do anything so radical or intellectually agile as put his reservations into words. He contented himself with scowling, which, all things considered, was probably his best move.

Vogel locked his slim nervous fingers together and smiled over them at Garen. Then he set about trying to impress on the man that this was a true bill, authorized from Washington, and that he had chosen Garen as the best man for the job. All of which was correct, as far as it went. Within his limitations Garen was still competent and reliable. He noticed Garen was wearing the uniform like a penitential smock, and suppressed a moment of impatience at the sight. Vogel tried to make a point of treating Garen with more forbearance than he would have shown other members of his staff. In fact he granted Garen the sort of uneasy consideration he might have extended to a cripple. Vogel was noted for his sharp tongue but he did not choose to employ it on Garen. Vogel used to say this was because he knew his limitations, but in fact the veteran agent both intrigued and disturbed him. Vogel sensed the spiritual confusion of the man, the sluggish resentments that curdled in him. He always tried to give Garen an easy ride, and was resigned to the fact that his manner would almost certainly be taken as evidence of condescension. Vogel knew there is a tribute success must pay to failure, intelligence to dullness. Nor did Vogel allow himself to forget that this gross figure had once been the executioner of Berlin. He had attained a certain status in the past. Garen interested him as a survivor, one of the brutal praetorians of the old regime. A good enough man for a bad time. The Agency should not be too eager to repudiate what it had once seen fit to call into being.

Sometimes Vogel would tell himself jokingly that the reason he kept Garen around was to make his flesh creep. Certainly all forms of grace wilted in Garen's presence. He had the rough charm of a bludgeon. In a curious way, Vogel did not want to let Garen go, though he knew he could expect no gratitude from him on that score. When the Departmental axe fell, Garen would certainly choose to believe that his retirement had been arranged by the young smart-ass of a superior who sat across the desk from him now. Vogel was not entirely sure what made him want to hang on to Garen. A well-read man, Vogel sometimes wondered whether he kept Garen around rather as the Pope was said to maintain a servant whose sole job was to whisper in his ear that he, too, was mortal and a sinner.

Vogel wound up his talk by stressing to Garen that this was the kind of job where the agent would be expected to make radio contact with headquarters at set hours. He knew what he was doing. In effect, Vogel was upgrading the operation, not because he foresaw any real danger to Professor Morrell, but in order to pacify Garen. By the time Garen left, he was even reconciled to the peaked cap. 'Set hours' was enough to make things all right. He was not being fobbed off, after all. He was still in business.

5

Arthur Morrell was enjoying his day in Oxford. He was enjoying it very much. From the beginning, it had taken on a triumphal air, right from the moment that Dr Bennett, the Master of his old College, came out to welcome him at the porter's lodge. Dr Bennett's manner had been courteous, but, more than that, it had been a quiet demonstration of the esteem which Morrell could now expect as his due. The thing was done in a civilized way but the message was clear. Arthur Morrell had gone up in the world, his stock stood high, and Dr Bennett made him aware of his new status with a few quiet words, a certain modest show of deference.

Morrell found that a room in the front quad had been put at his disposal, a pleasant room with moulded ceiling and casement windows that offered a view along what Morrell told himself must surely be one of the most famous streets in Europe. It was here that Morrell would do his robing and disrobing; here, too, that a sort of informal court began to be paid him soon after his arrival. Various people, some of them old colleagues, popped in to offer their congratulations and shake his hand. It was all very agreeable to Arthur Morrell.

He had also enjoyed the degree ceremony more than he expected. In the event, he got no sense of antiquated flummery from the occasion. He found it engagingly picturesque and decidedly impressive. The setting helped, of course, the measured elegance of the Sheldonian Theatre. Looking at the robed and furred dignitaries seated under the dome, Morrell could still only half believe that they had gathered there to honour him. He was not used to his celebrity yet, still eager for reassurance and grateful towards those who gave it, but humility of that kind could not be expected to last. Before long his new condition began to make other claims on him, starting with the address he gave to scientific colleagues later that day. He found his words receiving the special attention granted only to men of indisputable importance. This was gratifying, but in the course of his speech Morrell discovered a new and different source of pleasure, one that sprang from the secret duties he had undertaken for the United States government. Morrell reckoned he had pitched the speech pretty well. He was agreeably surprised to find how easily he could mask his various reticences with a show of candour. He did not see that there was any real question of dishonesty. He had gone as far as a man in his position could reasonably go. He had been scrupulous about withholding only the kind of information which ran counter to the demands of national security. It was the needs of security, rather than the demands of honesty, that now began to take over the forefront of Morrell's mind. Here, he sensed, was the crucial obligation he would be meeting in future.

So, Professor Morrell was led by his new eminence over the

border of deceit. His regard for scientific truth had begun to be coloured by political calculation – and he was immediately rewarded for that adjustment. He got a taste of that pleasure enjoyed at its keenest only by the great: the pleasure that comes from the justifiable suppression of truth, the deliberate mystifying of lesser men, who cannot, as a matter of policy, be let into the deepest secrets of the state. Worked on by the pressure of events and the susceptibilities of his nature, Arthur Morrell was moving towards a position where he would be able to countenance such behaviour, even in a scientist, accepting it as a natural obligation.

In fact, Arthur Morrell was saying goodbye that afternoon to the innocence of his scientific past. Politically, he had stopped being a victim, and what had led him to that position was not, in the final analysis, his superior intelligence, his good luck, nor any special taste for intrigue, it was his craving for approbation, his very human desire to be drawn into the circles of the elect.

Morrell's day in Oxford was scheduled to end with a private dinner-party in the Master's Lodgings, given in his honour by Dr Bennett. Afterwards, Garen would drive him to the airport and Mr Vogel would be present to see him safely on to the plane. It was all very satisfactory. He would go back to his researches – and to Judith. Several times during the course of the day he thanked Judith silently for understanding him so well. When he had hesitated about the Oxford trip, it was she who had urged him to make it. 'Who turns away honours?' she had said. 'You're an important man now, and you'd better get used to it. Go and see what people think of you.' It was the right advice. Oxford had been a very illuminating experience for him.

Morrell was also pleased by the way Garen had carried out his duties. The man had shown much more tact than his appearance might lead one to expect. Morrell's view about the need for Garen had also changed somewhat during the course of the day. Although he did not want any of his associates to become aware of the man's true role, he had begun to enjoy the idea of it himself. Garen had come to seem to Morrell like an emblem of his new status, living evidence that he was cherished by the high parental figures of the state.

6

Moishe drove the grey Rover out of London and took it some distance up the road to Oxford. He was alone in the car but David and Rachel were not far away: they were following in the black Mini David had hired that morning. A few miles beyond High Wycombe, Moishe pulled the Rover off the main highway and struck out along a secondary road which led them out into the Chiltern Hills. He could see through the driving-mirror that the Mini was still behind.

Moishe knew where to go. They had picked out the place already. The two cars climbed on to higher ground and after a few more miles they arrived at their destination. On the shoulder of a chalk hill there was a natural hollow. This hollow had been enlarged and flattened by bulldozers to make a picnic area. The place was meant to give motorists the advantage of a wide and pleasant view to the south while they paused to drink tea out of their Thermos flasks and open their foil-wrapped sandwiches. Now, with the tourist season over, the place was deserted, forlorn, its litter-baskets empty. The countryside below was gaining the poignancy of autumn: leaves were turning brown and golden in the copses; the grass had gone a more sombre green.

The Rover's tyres rolled over turf and white fragments of chalk. Moishe drove the car to the far corner of the parking area and brought it to a halt behind the toilet block, where it could not be spotted easily from the road. After locking the doors of his own car, Moishe climbed into the Mini, which was waiting nearby. Rachel had moved on to the back seat so that he could sit next to David. Moishe found himself wishing that he were doing the driving. David was a highly-strung sort of man and he was bound to be feeling nervous now, at the beginning of his first job. Moishe's particular worry was that, in a fit of nerves, David might make some stupid driving mistake, in which case the whole operation could conceivably end with them making statements to the local traffic-police. Moishe would have liked to suggest to David that he took the wheel, but he knew he could not do that without implying a lack of confidence in David which might be damaging to his self-esteem. Instead, Moishe suffered all the way to Oxford. He did not like being driven by other people at the best of times, and this was certainly not the best of times. What an outfit we are, he thought. Two greenhorns and a has-been!

They knew when the ceremony was taking place, so homing in on Morrell and the bodyguard presented no problem. All they needed was to confirm that the American professor had arrived in Oxford that morning to receive his degree. Once they had established that fact, they could allow Morrell to go about his business for the rest of the day. They knew his itinerary. The agent was the one that Moishe would be tagging, the thick-set man with the meat-grinder of a face. He needed to know the whereabouts of the Embassy car. Once he had the agent in view, Moishe told David and Rachel to go away until evening. 'Get lost, kids,' he said cheerfully. 'Just keep out of trouble, that's all.' He would rather they were out of sight for the next few hours. The move could not be made until Morrell was about to leave for the airport. In fact, he must *seem* to leave for the airport. No suspicions must be aroused. Secrecy was the hinge of this operation. Moishe arranged a place and time for the others to meet him again, and sent them on their way.

Seeing the agent in his chauffeur's uniform, Moishe could not help but grin. It was crude cover, but then they had no reason to expect trouble. Good enough for a routine job, that's how they must have argued it. Moishe tailed the agent, using the Mini when necessary, and the man never guessed. Moishe was glad to see the American car was equipped with a transmitter. He had banked on that. It was standard equipment. All the same, it was good to be right. Moishe smiled. Everything was falling into place.

David and Rachel lived through a day that grew stranger all the time. They knew Oxford very well. They had first met at university there. The place was full of memories for them : it brought to mind parties on scented summer's evenings, afternoons punting on the river, walks hand in hand through Christ Church meadows, concerts, cinemas, student productions of Shakespeare in floodlit College gardens. Untroubled days. Now they walked the streets of the city, David with a ·38 strapped under his arm, Rachel with a ·22 in her handbag, and the guns seemed to take away not just the innocence of the past, but its authenticity. As the clocks chimed the hours, it was as if the reality of Oxford were gradually leaking away. The city became insubstantial, all its old certainties set at nothing by the awesome presence of their guns, and the knowledge of what lay ahead. Towards the end they were marking off the time, minute by minute.

Garen had spent a boring day but he prided himself that he had done things right. He had been on hand to offer protection if any trouble arose. Nothing had happened, but that was no surprise to him. Ninety-nine times out of a hundred nothing did happen on a job like this. You only got action when you were sent out to make a hit. That kind of excitement would not be coming his way again. Garen thought wistfully of such occasions as another man might think of the pleasures of past love.

Garen did not have a high opinion of the town. His taste in architecture ran to the new, the stark, the colossal. He liked glass-and-concrete towers, buildings that punched holes in the sky. The Oxford Colleges looked puny and antiquated, like toy forts. Nor was he very much impressed by the academics. He cast a cold eye on the scholars in their scarlet cloaks and fur-trimmed hoods, as they filed into the Sheldonian. He had no use for old men in fancy dress.

Garen had put through the set calls on time. He had ferried Morrell to the hall where he was giving some sort of speech, and hung about in the foyer all afternoon in his goddam chauffeur's uniform. Waiting for the speech to end, Garen was driven to wonder, not for the first time in his life, how people could talk for so long. What the hell was there to *say*?

Once he had delivered Morrell back safely to the College, there was nothing else that could go wrong, not at least till they set off on the journey to the airport. The Professor had told him to report at 9.45 p.m. That meant Garen had time to kill. He had only one duty to perform before he collected the Professor and it was not something that would take long.

While Arthur Morrell dined with Dr Bennett and a party of Oxford notables, Garen passed his time in a public-house in Broad Street. He ate ham sandwiches and drank scotch on the rocks, but he was careful to go steady on the booze. The job was not over yet. Shortly before nine o'clock Garen lifted his broad backside off the stool, wondered whether to finish his drink, thought better of it and put the glass down again on the counter. 'Hey, Mac,' he said to the barman. 'Don't clear that away. I'll be back for it in a couple of shakes.'

The barman nodded.

Garen checked his watch and strode out of the pub. He was about to put in the last set call of the day. He had already decided it would be in order to make it from the parking lot. It had got pretty dark by now.

After the pub closed, the bartender found the glass still standing on the counter. The ice had long since melted into the whisky. He gave a shrug and tossed the stuff down the sink.

When Garen was drinking his slow glasses of scotch that

43

evening in the pub on Broad Street, his presence was known to Moishe and the others. They had met again and now were ready to go into action. David and Rachel lingered in the shadows on the corner, like a pair of lovers. Moishe was hunched over the wheel of the Mini. The moment they saw the agent framed in the light of the pub doorway, the others joined Moishe in the car.

As he walked down the street towards the parking lot, Garen did not notice the black Mini drive past him. There was no reason why he should.

At the entrance to the car park, a single slender column of concrete rose and arched like a swan's neck – the support for a sodium lamp which cast a bloodless glow on to the asphalt below. There was no other illumination. Beyond that, the darkness deepened, broken only by the slippery gleams of chromium, the pale bloom on the roofs of cars. At the far end of the lot there was a high wall, a solid line of darkness. A tree rose like a thunder-cloud above the wall, black against the faint haze of the city sky.

Garen felt no hint of danger. He walked heavy-footed among the sleeping shapes of cars to where his own vehicle stood, savouring the pleasure afforded by the workings of the whisky on his system. When the attack came, there was no more warning than a single footfall, the scrape of leather on grit. Garen had only time to feel a brief lurching bewilderment before the metal finger jabbed into the small of his back. A car nearby coughed and woke into life. The engine set up a steady throbbing that filled the silence. Garen did not try to fool himself. He understood the situation, and even before the voice spoke, he stopped walking. He knew with bitter certainty that he was standing at the wrong end of a gun. He had been jumped, which meant his head was on the block. There was mocking laughter somewhere in his skull.

'Hold it there!' The voice was so near to him that Garen felt breath strike warm against his cheek. He listened to the tone of the voice, noting the gutturals. It was a controlled voice, almost casual, the voice of a professional, with nothing in the pitch of it to give him hope. As he stood there, helpless, Garen was seized by a profound disgust at himself. The moment of his humiliation seemed to stretch out for ever. He saw what must follow. If not death, then the shabby room in Detroit, the old slob turned off in disgrace shuffling through the fag-end of his years. Garen was filled with such desperation that he almost wheeled round on the man then and there, but he restrained himself. Much better to play it along and wait his chance.

He tried not to wince, not to show his fear. He had done this kind of thing to others and he had sensed in them, beyond the terror of death, the special torment of the victim who knows that after his murder the assassin will go forward into some future where he can never hope to follow, never prosecute his revenge. Garen felt the bitterness of this thought now.

'Act naturally,' said the voice. 'Just do as you're told.' The words were barely audible, a murmur over the throb of the car engine.

'Yeah,' said Garen. 'Sure thing.' The gun ached against his backbone.

'Walk to your car now.'

As he stepped forward, Garen wondered whether he should take advantage of the movement to swing round and throw a punch at the man. It was a fantasy of resistance rather than the real thing. He would never have acted on it, even if the second guy had not showed himself. The second man came drifting out of the shadows on the right. At least Garen could see this one. A thin-faced punk with a long moustache. He had the look of some sort of dago. The dago made a point of letting Garen see that he was armed. Garen's eyes dwelt for a moment on the squat, stubby-barrelled gun. A Special. You couldn't argue with that. He would have to do as he was told, but he was not finished yet. Despair was giving way in Garen to a cold craftiness, he was not yet sure why.

'Unlock the car,' blurted the dago. 'Come on. Be quick!'

Could his moment have arrived already? Garen's right hand slid promptly inside his jacket.

'Hold it!' ordered the guttural voice. The gun jammed hard against his spine. Garen froze at once. 'Lift your hands clear. Let me see them.'

Garen let his arms dangle at his sides. He spread the fingers out. The stump waggled.

'All right. Now take it, David.'

'What? Take what? How do you mean?' The dago's eyes were round as saucers and his voice was shaking. He had the jitters. A novice. Garen stored the information away.

'The gun. Take his gun. He'll have one.'

Garen watched sourly while the nervous hands of the dago fumbled the Colt out of its holster. The real opposition stood behind him. He wished he could see the face of the leader, the man who was giving the orders.

'Open the door. Get aboard. Take the wheel.'

Garen did as he was told.

The two gunmen climbed into the back of the car. Garen tried to catch sight of the leader through the rear mirror. All he managed was a glimpse of pale hair and wide shoulders. For a moment he had been free from the gun. Now he felt it return, cold and hard. He heard it grate among the bristles at the base of his skull.

'Do exactly what you were going to do,' the guttural voice instructed him. 'And remember, we aren't playing games.'

Garen hesitated. He was finding it hard to think, but all the same certain conclusions were crystallizing in his mind: it struck him these people might have got things wrong. If they thought he was going to pick up Morrell now . . . He put his hands on the steering wheel and glanced at his watch. The luminous dial showed it was seven minutes past the hour. That meant the set call was already seven minutes late. Going by the book, the duty-man should have alerted Vogel by now. He drew in a sharp breath. Suddenly, there was hope.

'Whaddya mean?' asked Garen, making his voice slow, his tongue thick, like a man stupefied by fear. 'I was only going to pick somebody up.'

'Somebody? Not just somebody. You were going to pick up Professor Morrell!'

Garen gave a shiver of excitement. He kept a crafty silence.

'Weren't you?' The gun urged him to reply.

Garen tried to sound reluctant. 'The Professor? Yeah, that's right.' He pressed his knees together. They didn't know. They definitely didn't know! He felt a secret, savage joy. 'I'm just the driver,' he added, 'that's all.'

'We know what you are. Go on, then. Take the car. Pick up Morrell. But listen: one wrong move and you're dead. Don't get brave. Don't try to give Morrell any warning.' There was a pause. 'You understand what I'm saying?'

'Yeah,' mumbled Garen, aware of seconds ticking by. 'I don't want any trouble. Like I told you, I'm only the driver.'

'Where did he sit on the way up?'

'Sit?'

'What seat – front or back?' Garen could hear the snap of tension in the voice. The pressure mounted again on his neck.

'Came up in the back seat,' whispered Garen, holding very still.

'Right. Then you'll open the rear door for him. And see that he gets inside. Remember, one wrong move and Morrell will be dead. Your people won't like that, but at least you'll be in the clear. Know why? You'll be dead too.'

Tough hard-edged shit! thought Garen. Just let the time come and I'm going to enjoy taking you out.

'I shan't try nothing stupid, sir,' he whined. 'You can bet on that.'

The iron finger nudged him again. It poked into the folds of flesh that bulged over his collar. Garen understood. He obliged. He started the engine and swung the big limousine out of its rank towards the entrance. As he drove into the street, Garen saw he was being followed. Was it the other car, the one that had kept its engine running? The lights stayed with him all the way to the College. More of them, he thought. It struck him he could only see the lights because

47

there was nobody blocking the rear window now. The gunmen must be huddled down on the floor of the car. The muzzle of the gun was still at the base of his skull, but the angle of presentation had changed.

He brought the Embassy car to a halt in the box outside the College and watched the car behind drive past. As far as he could see there was only a dame at the wheel, so maybe he'd been mistaken. He was scared . . . anybody would be scared with a gun stuck in his neck, but Garen knew how the two in the back must be feeling, and that made up for a lot. It could only get worse for them from now on. Garen's face softened. He allowed himself a secret smile. They had a fair time to sweat it out. Twenty-five more minutes before Morrell was due to appear. Plenty could happen in twenty-five minutes.

Meanwhile, let these dudes keep sweating.

7

Vogel took up the enquiry himself. He had been informed, according to standard procedure, within five minutes of the agent's failure to register the call. It was probably nothing – and yet the matter could not simply be ignored. In terms of the manuals a failure such as this was deemed to constitute a preliminary alert. Vogel knew that Garen's silence was probably caused by something quite trivial. The trouble was, he couldn't be sure. If he didn't hear very soon, Vogel knew he would have to act. You could not take any chances in this business.

Normally, Vogel would have sent a subordinate to make the enquiry, but he was restless that evening, his thoughts turning back again to Africa. Besides, Vogel found he did not want to have another officer looking into Garen's failure. There was something uncomfortable for him about the idea. The bleary face drifted into his mind. As so often, the image of Garen struck Vogel with the force of a warning: 'Remember you too are mortal and a sinner.' Vogel tried to dismiss the feeling by indulging in a moment's annoyance. OK. Garen might not be quick, he might lack flair, but for Christ's sake, he was supposed to be reliable. The last word halted Vogel. He found he could not sustain his indignation. 'Reliable.' In how many cellars and back alleys, thought Vogel, beside what rotting warehouses and dark canals had Garen laboured to forge that sort of reputation? Reliable for what? There was an ugly certainty about the sort of demands which would be made on a man like Garen. And they had been made, for years. Until now he was not even fit for that role.

Vogel frowned, remembering the phrasing the directive had used about Morrell. It implied there was some very real importance to the scientist, an importance that was very little known about. Vogel wondered uneasily whether he had done the right thing in assigning Garen to this job. His response was to give orders for his car to be brought round. He would make the Oxford trip himself. He scribbled down the name of the College and shoved the scrap of paper into his breast pocket. How far was it to Oxford, anyway? Fifty miles? Something of that order. No distance at all. England was so cramped. Too little space, too many people.

He found himself following the same train of thought as he drove towards Oxford, weaving through the heavy traffic which choked the road, but it was not only England that could be relied upon to evoke Vogel's displeasure. He had long since fallen out of love with the entire Western technological culture he was hired to defend. Africa had done that for him. Africa, he thought, waiting for the lights to turn, Africa. He would never have guessed when he was first drafted into the squalor and blood-letting of the Congo that before long the continent would lay claim to his soul. With Lumumba dead and Mobutu finally installed, the Congolese operation had been regarded as a textbook example, a thoroughgoing

49

triumph for the West, and Vogel's part in these events had secured him an early reputation as a good man in the field. He came to be tagged as an expert on African matters. Deskmen in the States, relying on the information in their files, had kept him busy in one part or another of the continent for a good many years. That had been Vogel's great good fortune, the best thing that had ever happened to him. He had not once put in for a transfer from the African theatre, and when he was finally posted to Athens – to help bring on certain dubious politico-military changes – not all the Aegean lucidities of sea and sky had been able to lure his heart away from Africa.

It was not that he had any great love for black dictators. He did not take any keen pleasure in his mastery of tribal politics, nor did he find much to like in the raw, garish cities where concrete towers looked down on tin-roofed shanties. It was the interior of Africa which had captured Vogel's imagination, the vast hinterland which stretched like a province of memory, a huge dream out of the past. The wilderness, he thought, dodging about among the traffic. The wilderness! He got back there whenever he could. He knew many of the hunters and the wardens and counted them among his best friends. Vogel was at his happiest with them, lost in the emptiness of the *veldt*, wandering the grassy uplands. At first he had liked to hunt, but now he rarely shot any big game. He had come to realize how precariously the world of the great mammals survived, even in Africa. You could see the undiminished splendour of that world now only at some waterhole in the game reserves. Whereas man, he thought, as an advancing line of headlights swept across his eyes, man spawned endlessly. Man was infesting the earth. He looked at his wristwatch. The journey was taking him longer than expected. Vogel cursed the snarls of traffic.

Despite his new feeling for animals, occasionally when he went back to Africa, Vogel would take out a licence and go on a shoot. He was aware of the paradox of his behaviour, but not always able to resist the pleasure it offered. The killing of a great beast struck a deep resonance in him. There was a purity about it, a cleanness that was denied him in the tortuous proceedings of the Agency world – and yet it was not entirely unconnected with that world. Vogel might still kill game but, he thought defensively, it was a rare thing for him to do now. Mostly he was content to stay an observer. He might take photographs, but usually he did not even do that, he was happy merely to watch – apart from those exceptional moments when the need to mete out a clean death to some powerful creature would rise in him like a lust.

Vogel hung at the tail of a lorry and then swung out impatiently, taking a chance. He reminded himself that the last time he had levelled a gun at any sort of big game, the rifle had been loaded, not with a high-velocity bullet but a tranquillizing dart. He had gone out that day with his friend Ted Meakin, the assistant warden at Borozo, and their task had been to fix a sonic tag round the neck of a young lion so as to gain some definite information about its hunting range. Meakin had let Vogel make the shot. It had been an astonishing thing to watch. The big cat had fallen down and lain still as death and you could go up to it and put your hand upon its head, examine the daggers of its teeth, run the coarse hairs of the black mane between your fingers, lift up the huge paws. Of course, you could do all these things with a beast you had killed, and that was an awesome experience, but this time it had been even more tremendous because what Vogel had dispensed was not only death but resurrection. Once Ted had fixed the bleeper on the lion's neck, they retreated to the Land-Rover and after a while they saw the twitching of the lion's flanks. The beast yawned, stretched, found its feet and went ambling away. It was somehow prodigiously significant to Vogel to think that he had stood close to the unconscious creature and laid his hand upon its head and taken no harm.

'Oxford Ten Miles' said the sign.

When Vogel's leaves came around, he did not make for the fun-cities of Europe or America. He took the plane back to Africa. He was due for some time off soon and had been dreaming up his next expedition when the news came through about the call. As he pushed on towards Oxford he tried to let his thoughts stay with the elephants of the Ituri Forest, but he could not escape a sense of uneasiness. Vogel had an instinct for trouble, and now, like a faint distant clamour, it began to make itself heard in the depth of his being.

8

David was crouching beside Moishe in the back of the car. The palms of his hands were clammy, his throat dry, and there was a kind of numbness in his head, as if some vessel in there had burst and was clogging his brain with blood. It was the waiting that was doing the damage, he realized that. None of them had foreseen this awful dragging delay. When they had made their plans, they had leapt easily past this moment. It was a simple matter : Morrell came out and they took him. But now Morrell refused to play his part. He would not come. The waiting was like having your resolve set against a grindstone and watching it slowly wear away. It was not only the waiting, it was having to wait here, at the very doors of the College. If was as if the car were balancing on the edge of a cliff. Worst of all, it was being cooped up with Morrell's bodyguard, having to endure this kind of suspense in face of the man's sullen hostility.

David stared at the wary back, the shaven neck with Moishe's pistol lodged against its bulging flesh. Death was actually touching the man in the front seat. It had set a cold hard finger against his skin. Surely he must be suffering too, though he showed no sign. David had been startled by the threats he had heard Moishe make. During their planning, David had never allowed himself to believe there might really be killing. Now he saw how easily it could come to that. He felt an urge to pray, as if that might lessen the chance of murder, but he could find no words. His thoughts turned to Rachel. She would have parked the Mini by now and be waiting for them to come and pick her up. David could imagine her standing on the corner, peering down the road, her face pinched under the blonde wig. He endured her anxiety as well as his own.

An infinite time passed – ten minutes by his watch. Why in God's name didn't the American appear? He felt Moishe stir beside him. 'Come on, Morrell,' Moishe growled. 'Get a move on, damn you!' He shoved the muzzle of the gun deeper into the neck of the man in the driving seat. 'Hey, you! Where's Morrell? Why isn't he here?'

The big shoulders gave a slight shrug.

'You told us the truth?'

'Sure I did.' The man spoke carefully, without turning his head. 'He ought to be here by now. It's past his time.'

'And this is the right place? This is where you were to pick him up?'

'Yeah.'

'You're certain?'

'That was my orders. To come here.'

'Man!' said Moishe. 'You'd better be telling the truth!'

More minutes dragged by. David felt the tension mounting in him. 'What do we do?' he blurted. 'I mean, what do we do if . . .'

'Do?' Moishe cut in, stung by the question. 'Do? We wait. That's all we can do.'

David heard his voice go babbling on. 'Maybe there's been a change of plans. Maybe Morrell's staying here . . .'

'Maybe. Maybe. Who knows? Maybe doesn't help.'

'Does that mean . . . ? We shan't have to call it off, shall we?' There was longing as well as anguish in David's voice. He heard it and was ashamed.

Moishe gave a sigh. 'Shut up, cousin,' he said.

But David couldn't stop the questions coming. 'If we have

53

to call it off – what about him?' He pointed to the man with
the gun at his neck.

'Ah,' said Moishe. 'Him.'

David fell silent, his heart heavy. But then a strange thing
happened. His mood changed, as if he had gone beyond the
farthest point of fear, had suffered the worst it could do to
him, and now was set free from it. As if fear had first sought
him out and then abandoned him. He felt a determination
he had never expected. His release came on him like a gift,
like the sudden descent of grace. He was astonished.

He heard Moishe's voice: 'Somehow or other we have to
get Morrell out of there.' Moishe was talking mostly to himself.
'We can't hang around all night.'

'Listen,' said David. 'I'll go in.'

'You? Go in there?'

'Why not? We must do something.'

'You?' said Moishe again, and David felt the pale eyes rest
on his face. He knew Moishe had sensed the change in him.
He seemed to accept its reality. Maybe it was something
Moishe had seen happen to men before.

'And it has to be me that goes in,' David went on. 'I'm the
only one who knows the College. I could snoop around. I'll
fetch Morrell back for us.' He found he was eager to go. 'We
don't get another chance, Moishe,' he urged.

'And you think you'd be capable of such a thing?'

'I think I have to try.'

There was a moment's pause while Moishe considered.
'Sure,' he said at last, 'you're right.' He raised his free hand
and pressed David's shoulder. It was a moving gesture, the
kind of salute a man makes to a comrade. 'And I'm here,'
said Moishe. 'Remember that. If you run into trouble, I'll be
here. Both of us will still be here.' He nodded towards the
hulking figure in the front seat. 'That fellow might have his
uses then.' He gave a grin. The prospect of action, the hope
of finding some way out of their impasse, had awoken a sense
of exhilaration in them both. David noticed how Moishe's
eyes glittered in the dim light of the street lamp. He got out

54

of the rear door of the car. 'Back soon,' he said.

David walked with what he hoped was a casual air through the entrance of the College and into the quadrangle. He wondered whether to go and ask after Professor Morrell at the porter's lodge, but decided against it, at least for the time being. Better if he did not have to speak to anybody. He knew the College well. It was only a few years since he had been an undergraduate here. He guessed that Morrell would be using the set of rooms usually reserved for well-known visitors. He knew the whereabouts of those rooms. Number three staircase, ground floor. That had to be his first objective.

He walked around the quad. There were lighted windows, golden rectangles piercing the dark masonry. From somewhere overhead came a peal of tipsy laughter. The walls of the quadrangle held the air still. As always, it was like being under a glass dome.

David examined his feelings. He remained astonished by them. He had found that he did not lack courage, which meant his worst nightmare had been routed. He was not a coward. He was not afraid. Indeed, he was enjoying a curious emotional freedom. His mind was swept clear of the worries of ordinary life. The heat of this one great undertaking seemed to have melted them all away. His thoughts, which had been dulled before by the weight of blood in his skull, were now lucid and sharp – his brain had come back wholly into his service. Wonderful! As a biologist, David understood the scientific explanation of the matter. He was high on a lavish charge of adrenalin. He saluted the fact, but with playful zest. Such a system! Such miracles of body chemistry! All the same, the confidence did not feel like a glandular stratagem, it seemed more as if spiritual support had arrived. He was filled with the conviction that they would succeed. More than that, he, David Schuster, would make sure they did. Every step he took towards the staircase became a cause for greater satisfaction. He would never have believed there was so much boldness in his nature.

The windows of the rooms at the foot of staircase three

showed no light. David glanced quickly round. At that moment, the quad was empty. He drifted through the arched entry and gently tried the door. It swung open. This did not surprise him. Doors in Oxford Colleges were rarely locked. The room beyond lay in darkness. David slipped inside and closed the door. He forced himself to remain still for a few moments while his eyes grew used to the dimness. All he could hear was the pumping of his heart, a series of blows against the wall of his chest, a steady muffled drum. The street lamp cast some light through the outer window, but it was a lurching inconstant illumination, speckled with shadows, strung with limbs of blackness. There was a tree between the window and the lamp, its leaves flickering, its branches swaying in the wind. David looked round the room. There was a briefcase on the desk. Papers. An overcoat draped across a chair. David tried the briefcase. It was locked, but on the leather below the brass lock were stamped the initials A.M. He lifted the papers to the light. Notes for a speech on gene-expression. David gave a grin. He had guessed right. These things were the personal property of Arthur Morrell. No doubt Morrell would be coming back to collect them. And soon. David took the ·38 out of his shoulder-holster, weighed the gun thoughtfully, then slid it into his jacket pocket. As he stood in the darkness, debating his next move, he heard the sound of footsteps outside. There was a hand fumbling with the knob of the door.

He moved quickly then.

9

Arthur Morrell was obliged to take leave of the dinner-party while the port was still going round. He had told Dr Bennett and the others not to disturb themselves on his account, indeed he had insisted that they should not. As he explained, he had only to pick up a couple of things from his room and he would be on his way. His chauffeur, he told them, smiling, should have brought the car round to the door by now. When Dr Bennett made as if to see him out, Morrell declared that he wouldn't hear of such a thing. He was very definite. Nobody should be disturbed at table because of him. He was sorry he had to dash away but there was a plane to catch and these things would not wait. Morrell's consideration was so determined that after only a slight show of protest, Dr Bennett bowed to his wishes. Besides, neither he nor any of the other elderly gentlemen round the table was particularly eager to exchange the warm room for a draughty few minutes in the College porch.

Afterwards, as the port went round again, some observations were made about the curiously thrusting nature of transatlantic manners. At the same time, it was generally conceded that, in his field, Arthur Morrell was an excellent man and the College should be proud of the connection.

The scholars showed their own sort of consideration to Morrell, confining themselves to only a few sly shafts of malice at his expense.

Morrell was flattered by the way his opinions had been received that evening. He felt *justified* to the depths of his being. As he put it to himself, the food had been excellent, the company more so. The wine helped complete his feeling of happiness. He strode across the quad, buoyed up by a sense of achievement. Life felt very good.

Morrell entered the guest-room, flicked on the light and went over to the window to check whether Garen had brought the car round yet. Through the branches of the tree, he could make out the black limousine by the College gates. Garen was sitting at the wheel. Excellent!

As he walked towards the desk, Morrell became aware of a movement somewhere behind him. He turned to find himself looking at a dark thin young man who was leaning against the wall.

Morrell was startled enough to back away a couple of paces.

'You surprised me,' he said, trying to recover his poise. 'What are you doing here?'

The young man offered him a smile as if to say, You will hardly believe what I am doing here. He seemed hesitant but his brown eyes belied his tentative manner. The eyes shone with inexplicable enthusiasm.

Morrell tried again: 'What is it you want?'

'I need to talk to you, Professor Morrell.'

'Talk to me? What about?'

'Some of the implications of gene-expression.'

'Oh.' Morrell smiled, though he was not entirely at ease. 'I'd very much like to, but I'm afraid I have a plane to catch. So it won't be possible.' It had just struck Morrell that the young man must have been standing there in the dark, waiting for him. Could this be a thief? No, no, thought Morrell. A thief was hardly likely to be conversant with the terms of micro-biology, not even in Oxford. He offered the young man another smile.

The young man returned it.

'Well, that's that then.' Morrell turned away. 'I'm afraid I have to go.'

'I shall be coming with you, Professor.' The soft voice sounded terribly confident.

Morrell stood up very straight. He was a big man, much bigger than the intruder, and he sought to draw this fact to the young man's attention. 'I can't begin to understand what you mean,' he said coldly.

'What I mean is . . . Oh, why don't you just get your things together? It's time we were on our way.'

Morrell frowned, hesitated, then tried to bluff. 'Look here,' he said, 'I don't know you, I've got no business with you, and if you don't leave this room at once, I'm afraid I . . .' but as he spoke, he remembered Garen and the reason for Garen's presence and his voice died away. And though his mouth fell open at the young man's next move, somewhere deep inside him he was not entirely surprised. The man took a revolver out of his pocket and pointed it at Morrell's chest. Morrell flinched, aware that in these new circumstances his size had turned into a disadvantage.

'What is it you want?' he asked huskily. 'Money? Do you want money?' He began to feel for his wallet.

The young man was brisk, affable, but there was a definite note of menace in his voice now. 'Keep your hands where I can see them! Gather your things, Professor Morrell. Please do as I say. Don't bother to argue. We have no time to lose.' He gestured with the gun.

Morrell nodded. He saw that calamity had entered his life. Part of him had always expected it. He picked up his briefcase, put on his overcoat, hardly knowing what he was doing.

'And the papers.'

'They're . . . no longer wanted,' said Morrell. He was humble now.

'Just bring them.'

Morrell did as he was told. His thoughts turned towards his bodyguard. Did the gunman know about Garen? Morrell felt the birth of a sort of hope, but he was afraid of the hope, too, scared of what it might entail.

'Listen carefully,' said the young man. 'We shall be leaving the College together, Professor. We shall talk as we go on some scientific subject. Let's make it plasmids. You will say goodbye to the porter and you won't forget to give him the usual tip. Right? If you try to indicate that you're in any sort of trouble – I shall be obliged to shoot you. Is that understood?'

Morrell licked his lips, nodded. There was a dreadful lilt to the young man's voice. It frightened him.

'Let's go,' said the gunman. 'Now, about plasmids . . .'

They walked out of the College together. The young man did most of the talking, but now and then Morrell drove himself to make some contribution. At the lodge, he managed a hoarse goodbye to the porter and put a five-pound note on the counter. The porter wished him a pleasant journey but gave him no more than a fleeting glance, most of his attention being centred, naturally enough, upon the money.

There stood the car, beyond the gateway. Just across the road an old man in a raincoat was walking a Dalmatian. Although the man and the dog were so near, Morrell felt an impassable gulf divided him from them. He wondered again about Garen.

They reached the car and Garen climbed out of the driver's seat to open the rear door. Morrell gave his bodyguard a fierce, enquiring glance. 'Better get in, Professor,' said Garen. He sounded tired. Garen did not seem to need any explanation of the young man's presence nor, obviously, was he going to challenge it.

When Morrell got into the car, he found there was another of them in the back, another man crouched in the shadows. Morrell felt a gun poke into his ribs and his hopes of rescue died. There was not going to be any escape from this nightmare.

The dark young man sat beside Garen. 'We have another passenger to pick up,' he said. 'Drive on till you see a young woman standing by the kerb. A blonde. I'll tell you the right woman.'

Garen gave a grunt.

Just as the car started, the man in the back spoke. 'You did well, David,' he said in a throaty voice. 'My God, you did well!'

Morrell did not dare turn his head.

10

Vogel did not know Oxford very well, but he had enough knowledge of the town to persuade himself that he could find his way to the College. He was wrong. He got lost. After being caught in a network of one-way streets, Vogel found himself being funnelled back on to the London road. He was annoyed at his mistake. It had cost him several minutes and in the end he had been forced to ask a policeman the way.

Vogel reached the College just in time to see the big black Embassy car pull away and pass him on the other side of the road. His first feeling was one of relief. Everything was OK. Then his brain registered the fact that there had been too many passengers. The clamour of alarm sounded fiercely in his head. There seemed to have been four of them in the car. Four men. Something had to be wrong.

Vogel looked for a place to turn. By the time he had got himself facing the right way, the Embassy car had gone round the corner and he was afraid he might have lost it. His foot went down hard and he pushed through the traffic-lights just as they turned red. A moment later he had to stand on his brakes. The Embassy car had pulled in by the kerb a little way ahead and was taking on another passenger. What the hell *is* this? thought Vogel. He supposed it was just possible that Morrell was stopping voluntarily to pick up a blonde – the man had a reputation in that field. It was possible, but it was damned unlikely. Besides, Garen knew better than to take any passengers aboard. Vogel wondered whether it had been Garen at the wheel. He thought he had seen the shiny peak of a chauffeur's cap, so it looked as if Garen was still doing the driving. Under duress, then? Duress, he thought bleakly. A fancy word for men with guns, men with knives. Vogel's nostrils flared at the thought. He pressed his lips together. At least, he told himself by way of comfort, his luck had held. Another minute and they'd have got clean away.

Tagging them down the main highway was not hard but after about twenty miles the Embassy car turned off into a country lane which was almost empty of traffic. Vogel had to hang a long way back now, driving on dip. He watched the shifting glare of the lights ahead as they picked up trees and hedges. The move into the country left Vogel in no doubt: Morrell was in deep trouble. The certainty of it calmed him. He became almost serene.

The road led into a range of low hills. Vogel noticed the lights ahead suddenly swing over to the left, as if the car were pulling off the road. The lights remained still for a moment, shining on a white wall of chalk, a scar on the hillside. Then they went out. The car had stopped. Why? Maybe, thought Vogel, there was a barn or a farmhouse in the hollow, some place that could be used as a hide-out. That made the best sense – which didn't mean it was the right answer. Vogel took his car as close as he dared, groping forward, using sidelights only. He stopped in the entry to a field-gate, which left him with about a hundred yards still to cover. From this point he would have to make his way on foot.

Vogel took a pair of field-glasses out of the glove compartment and let his right hand rest for a moment on his gun. Then he vaulted over the gate and set off up the field. He was on the shoulder of a hog's-back hill. There was springy turf underfoot. He climbed quickly to the top of the rise. From there, with any luck, he would have a view down on to the place where the car had stopped. But he had to be quick. There was no knowing what might be going on below. Vogel did not think it likely that they meant to kill Morrell – they could have done that without bringing him so far. All the same, you never knew. There were some crazy characters around. He found himself wishing he knew why Morrell was important.

Vogel made it to the top of the rise and saw a couple of cars standing below him in a big hollow. No farm, no barn. The place stretched like an empty stadium. The roof light was burning in the Embassy car and things were going on inside there. Vogel focused the glasses. He could make out Morrell and Garen now. Also a gun in somebody's hand. The hand with the gun was not far from Garen's head. Vogel frowned, trying to figure out what the scene meant and decide on his next move.

11

Rachel looked at David and Moishe. Their faces were different. They seemed like cats' faces, intent, the eyes staring. The way they spoke was different, too. There was more than tension in their voices. They grated. They had gone ugly and cold. Rachel had not foreseen this and her heart beat fast. She had not understood that David and Moishe would be so changed by what they were doing.

So far, everything had gone as planned, and Rachel was glad of that, yet it had all turned out very different from anything she had expected. It was the violence that she had left out of account. Before, when she imagined these events, she had always pictured them in heroic terms, but what surrounded her now was violence, deliberate terror. She felt lost among frightening strangers. The repeated threats of death rang in her head. 'Do it!' Moishe had snarled at the bodyguard, only a few moments before. 'Do it, or I'll blow a hole through your skull!' Meanwhile ramming the muzzle of his gun into the man's ear, actually forcing it hard against the whorls of gristle. The agent had dwindled down, he had seemed to shrink physically under the threat. And Morrell had sat watching this performance, eyes staring, cheeks livid, keeping absolutely still, with David smiling at him. It was a smile such as she had never seen on David's face before.

Rachel grew angry at her thoughts and told herself not to be so feeble. She took the ·22 out of her handbag as if to prove her determination. She was willing to go wherever David and Moishe led. Heroism might be darker and more forbidding than she had imagined; nevertheless, it remained heroism. She had to believe that. David and Moishe were doing what must be done.

63

Once they had forced the bodyguard to open the radio link with the Embassy, Rachel felt things got less bad. The violence was, in a sense, directed to the other end of the line. The blows were dealt and suffered at long range.

Rachel listened to Moishe. He was speaking into the transmitter. She heard him say: 'We have got Morrell. And the man who is with him. The guard. You understand?' He repeated the information. 'You will realize,' he added with a triumphant flourish, 'that this is a subject on which I should like to speak to the Ambassador.'

A pause followed and then Moishe's conversation with the Ambassador began. Moishe's voice had a passionate confidence; the Ambassador answered in nipped terms, his voice flat, his tone guarded. He asked for proof and Morrell was called upon to provide it.

Morrell's voice shook. It was strained and ragged. 'Morrell here,' he said. 'Professor Arthur Morrell. It's true, Ambassador. You have to believe me. Kidnapped. Yes. And they're armed, Ambassador. They have guns.'

There was a silence, followed by a squawk as the Ambassador cleared his throat. This was the nearest the Ambassador came to any show of emotion. Finally he said, 'May I know your terms?' and his voice was bloodless.

This was a moment of triumph for them. 'Listen,' said Moishe. 'Listen.' He gave a breathless laugh. 'Listen very, very carefully. You have a direct line to the White House?'

The Ambassador kept a pained silence.

'You are going to open that line immediately, Ambassador. You are going to speak direct to your President. Tell him about Professor Morrell. The news must be kept very private. Don't discuss it with anyone else.'

'I can't see that . . .'

'I should do as you are told, Ambassador. I think you'll find that Professor Morrell is very highly valued by your government. He's worth a great deal.'

'The terms? What are the terms?'

'Ah, yes. The terms. They can be found at the Central

Post Office in Washington.'

'I beg your pardon?'

'You heard me. The President must send a personal aide at once to the Central Post Office in Washington. The man will go to Box 458. Have you got that? PO Box 458.'

'Yes.'

'Please repeat the number to me. There must be no mistake.'

The Ambassador did so, speaking with heavy distaste.

'Inside the box there is a sealed envelope. This must be given *unopened* into the President's hands. It is essential that the envelope should go direct to the President. Inside, he will find our terms for the release of Professor Morrell.'

'Have you finished?' asked the Ambassador. 'Is that it?' He sounded drained. When this humiliating phone call was over, he knew he would have an even worse one to make.

'Just make sure you get it right, that's all.' As he spoke, Moishe seized Morrell by the collar and dragged him forward over the seat. 'Tell him,' said Moishe, putting his gun to Morrell's head. 'Tell him to do as I say.'

'Please,' grunted Morrell, half-choking. 'I beg you, Ambassador . . .'

Moishe let go of Morrell and turned off the transmitter. 'Right,' he said. 'That does it! Let's get to the other car.'

Rachel felt a deep sense of relief now that this part of the business was over. They had taken the biggest step. Surely there would be less need for violence now? She climbed out of the Embassy car. The air was cool and fresh. The moon had risen. It cast a dim foggy light from behind cloud. Just beside her was David, holding the bodyguard at gun-point. Moishe followed, bringing up the rear with Morrell. She heard the doors of the Embassy car swing shut and she was glad. Rachel was anxious to get back to the Rover. She wanted to leave the strangeness behind her in the strange car. She walked on, the ·22 clutched in her fist.

Suddenly, there was a confused flurry, a swirl of movement. Arms swung. She heard David cry out, watched him go down under the fists of the bodyguard. A second later the bodyguard lunged out for her. His hand came down on her shoulder like a great paw and she twisted away from under it. Whether it was from fear or, as she afterwards suspected, from a kind of instinctive calculation, Rachel chose that moment to drop her gun. She knew that, at all costs, she must not let the body-guard get her. If that happened, they were finished. So, on a gamble, she dropped the gun. It clonked on the stony ground.

All his adult life Garen had put his trust in guns. He had been taught long since that, without a gun, a man was nothing. When they took away his Colt earlier that night he had felt himself horribly diminished. Now, with the chance of getting his hands on a gun again, nothing else mattered. He bent down to gather the ·22 and allowed Rachel to escape round the far side of the Rover.

A moment of great confusion followed. Rachel heard David groan and Moishe shout, 'Lie flat!' There was a flash and the bang of a gun going off. For a moment Rachel thought David had been shot and a murderous rage sprang up in her. She could have killed the bodyguard then. If she had been holding a weapon, she would have emptied it into him.

By the dim light of the moon, she saw the bodyguard turn and run. He went zigzagging away, making for the entrance to the parking area. As he ran he shouted something, the meaning of which escaped her. She suffered a moment of dreadful suspense, before she heard David's voice. 'Moishe. I'm OK!' Then Rachel began to shake. Her legs were so weak she had to lean on the car. Her head was swimming.

When Rachel recovered, David and Moishe were muttering together in low, guarded voices. 'No, we can't let him do that,' Moishe was saying. 'Besides, he's not going to run. He's got us boxed in.'

She watched Moishe hand Morrell into David's keeping and then saw him go stealthily round the far side of the toilet block. The silence hung heavy. Rachel and David looked into each other's faces. The moon had broken free of cloud now and was peering down on them like some huge round

66

enquiring eye. The waiting went on. Morrell stood beside them, half-forgotten. Under the moon, the banks of earth by the entrance looked peaceful. There was no sign of life among them.

When the reports came, Rachel jumped violently. There were two shots close together. Almost at once, Moishe came back into sight. He was walking quickly.

When Moishe reached the others he handed Rachel back her gun without comment. 'Now we really have to get away fast,' he said. 'The noise could bring somebody.'

Moishe's words awoke in all of them a frantic haste to be gone. They piled into the Rover. This time Moishe took the wheel and Rachel and David sat in the back with Morrell between them. Rachel could feel Morrell pressed against her. He was shaking.

As the Rover swept out of the parking area its headlamps picked out a shape on the side of the road. Rachel did not understand at first what it was.

'Dead?' she heard David ask huskily.

'What else?' said Moishe. He sounded aggrieved. 'What else could be done? He was staked out, waiting for us. A crazy man!'

'You're leaving him there? Shouldn't we . . . ?'

'No time,' said Moishe. 'We have no time, cousin. We must get clear. Everything depends on that.'

Rachel listened to the urgent voices. She remembered how they had ringed the man's face in the photographs, and how threatened she had felt at the sight of those brutal features. Now it seemed as if they had been marking out the bodyguard for destruction. But that was not true. He was the one who had tried to do the killing. He had meant to shoot David. The knowledge closed up her heart against him. She thought of the huddled corpse lying by the side of the road. So that was a killing. She had not expected it to be like that. The corpse looked like nothing very much. A heap of old clothes. You could drive past such a thing and never notice. The idea troubled her. It was hard to believe that a man could be brought down in an instant to a mere bundle of rags. The thought made her want to put her arms round David and hold him close, but she could not reach him. Morrell sat between them. Shaking.

12

Through the glasses, Vogel watched Garen make his move. The move was like the man – crude, dangerous, lacking subtlety. Vogel cursed under his breath, watching Garen pick up the girl's revolver and fire it. He saw Garen go running towards the entrance and heard the strangled bellow that forced its way past Garen's lips: 'No more shit! I'm taking no more shit!'

Like the bull, Vogel had time to think. Like the fighting bull when the picadors stick their lances in his neck – and we know how that story ends! As he made this sour reflection, Vogel jumped to his feet and began to sprint down the field towards his car. He tried to get some order into his thoughts. He knew he had to find a way of stopping this business before the gunplay really got going. Garen's action had certainly put Morrell at risk. Vogel must somehow try to retrieve the situation. But how? He would have to play the thing by ear. There was no easy way.

As Vogel took his car on to the road, headlights went raking across the hedgerows up in front. When he saw this, the frown cut deeper between Vogel's brows. He pushed along the road, moving fast, and almost failed to see Garen. He stopped beside the body. The lights threw a pallid glare on Garen's face. Vogel could see at a glance that the man was dead, mouth open, eyes staring, unprepossessing in death as in life. Vogel peered after the lights, trying to work out the speed at which the car was making its way down the valley. He reckoned he had a couple of minutes in hand. Just as well. Garen could not be left on the roadside for local people to find next morning.

Vogel scrambled out of the car, flung open the rear door and ran to Garen. He worked his hands under the man's armpits. Garen was still warm and he was very heavy. As Vogel crouched over him, he saw the hole in Garen's chest. It needed all his strength to haul the corpse back to the car. Come on, you big ox, he thought with anguish, you big, dumb, clumsy ox, forcing the legs in, bending the knees so that he could get the door shut. Vogel whipped off his raincoat and threw it over the body, making sure that the face was covered. He looked up, panting. The business hadn't taken long : he could still see the lights of the other car moving down the valley. Vogel made haste to narrow the distance between himself and the lights.

Once he had closed up on them, he was confident he could hold them. Driving behind the Rover, Vogel pondered on the way they had finished Garen. The bullet had gone straight through Garen's heart. So – experts. It looked as if Morrell must have fallen into the hands of experts. Efficient and ruthless operators, as Garen's body proved. That was the scene.

But there was one important fact those experts did not know, thought Vogel, and it was his business to make sure they did not get to know. They did not realize that another expert was sitting on their tail.

13

Moishe drove them without trouble to the house in West London. Rachel opened the wooden gates and Moishe took the Rover lurching over the potholed tarmac of the drive.

They put the Rover away in the garage and went into the house. While these things were taking place, Morrell did all that he was told.

Soon they were standing blinking in the light of the first-floor living-room. They could see each other's faces clearly for the first time since they had made the snatch. Looking at each other, they began to laugh and shake their heads in disbelief. Their laughter came as a surprise to them, and that made them laugh all the more.

David punched Moishe's arm. 'Done it!' he exclaimed, his eyes filling. 'Cousin, we have actually done it!' He spread his arms out wide, as if to show the huge size of their success.

'Yes,' said Moishe. 'We should have a drink on that, *chaverim*.' He went over to the cupboard and came back with three glasses and a couple of flagons of beer. As he poured each of them a drink, Moishe saw Rachel glancing in Morrell's direction. He shrugged. 'We can hardly ask *him* to join us,' he said, and they all began to laugh again. They toasted their good fortune, the success of the cause. Nobody mentioned the dead man left lying by the road. Moishe had explained it to them on the way back: in a war, there were casualties; casualties were best forgotten. Moishe hoped the others would take his advice, though. He had never been able to take it himself. There were many things Moishe could not forget.

Morrell stood outside the circle, ignored by them. He did not yet dare look directly at his captors. He had the air of a very shy man at a party.

'Go away now, kids,' said Moishe when the beer was finished. 'Go off by yourselves. I'll take first watch. No, I insist.' He was at his most benign, waving them away, offering them an ironical blessing.

Rachel signalled with her eyes. She held out her hands towards David.

'And try to get some sleep, eh?' Moishe called after them. 'You'll have to stand your guard, too, don't forget. OK,' he added, spreading his hands, hunching his shoulders, acting the reasonable man, 'try to get some sleep *as well*.' He gave them a big wink. Excitement showed in his every word, his every gesture. Moishe knew that later the reaction would set in, but he was not there yet. He was still flying high.

Once they were in the bedroom, Rachel put her arms round David, as she had so much wanted to do earlier, but he put her gently aside. First, he had to pray.

He made his affirmation of the Holy One and then went on to ask God's forgiveness, speaking out loud so that Rachel could hear what he was saying. Any blood that had been shed, he asserted, had not been shed by their choice. Their cause must be their warrant. Like the Sons of Mattathias, they had taken up arms to prevent the destruction of Israel. He went on to give thanks to God for the gift of courage. Rachel listened to him with awe. She could not help remembering the harsh changes she had seen take place in David that night, but when he came to her arms, he was the same gentle David as always. These complexities of being weighed on her. She and David lay still for a long time. Then they made love.

Moishe sat in the living-room, his long legs sprawled out, a drink in one hand and his gun in the other. He was looking at Arthur Morrell and wondering how he felt. Pretty awful, he imagined. Moishe debated whether to offer the scientist a glass of beer. Morrell sat across from him, staring fixedly down at the floor. For a long time neither of them spoke.

With Morrell safely in their hands, Moishe was experiencing some relief at last from the desperate frustration he had endured so long. He remembered the baffled rage that had consumed him after the Bureau pensioned him off and he was left to try to ignore his fears and seek a foothold again in ordinary life. He might have gone to his father for help and comfort, but Jacob Hartmann was dead by then, and without his father's presence, Moishe felt unable to bear the austere, blinkered simplicities of kibbutz life. With his brother Simon also long dead, Moishe had turned to the other surviving member of his family, his sister Emmie. He had lived for some months in the smart Tel Aviv apartment of Emmie and her husband, a moon-faced citrus exporter called Reuben, and listened hopelessly to their endless chatter about the children, the television, the car, the latest gadgets for the kitchen, the luxury bathroom they hoped to install. Blind inane banalities! Emmie and Reuben liked everything to be nice and did not want to hear any talk of an unpleasant nature.

It was from this base that Moishe had struggled to gain a foothold in ordinary life. He had taken a job as a car salesman in the showrooms of Mr Hertzel. Oh, the misery and frustration of those months! One day Moishe could stand no more of it. He picked up a crowbar and laid about the premises of his employer. The Bureau had shielded him from prosecution – they discouraged publicity about men like Moishe – and directed him to a psychiatrist. Moishe had surrendered himself to the psychiatrist, who urged him to disclose his most private fears. When Moishe told him about the helpless rage he felt, seeing his country being manœuvred towards destruction, the psychiatrist had written in his notebooks the words 'paranoid obsession'.

After a number of interviews, the psychiatrist reached the astonishing conclusion that Moishe was on the verge of a breakdown and prescribed rest for him in the shape of a quantity of yellow pills. He also suggested that Moishe should travel and get a change of scene. Moishe despised this advice but found himself taking it. The pills he threw down the lavatory, but he left Israel and began wandering up and down Europe – not so much travelling as despairingly pacing the floor of his cage.

This had been his mood when he returned to England and met his cousin, David, again. If it had not been for that visit, undertaken on the weakest of impulses, he would still have been racking his brains for some way of striking back. Moishe found his cousin greatly changed. As a deeply committed Zionist, David shared his fears, but more than that, David was an educated man, a scientist. He had contacts among clandestine groups of zealots in the universities of Britain and

America. That had been the vital connection. The secret information had been passed to them from America and David's training as a micro-biologist had allowed him to grasp the momentous possibilities of the thing. They had gone on from there. The plan was entirely their own. They had called on others only for that one small but vital service at the Central Post Office in Washington. It had seemed a crazily ambitious scheme – but now, with Morrell beside him, Moishe could believe they would succeed. He warmed himself at Morrell's presence like a man, chilled to the bone, might stand before a blazing fire.

Outside, Vogel was on the prowl. He felt he had the situation well in hand now. Some of his best men were already on their way. He had given instructions about picking up the Embassy car. Garen's body would be removed before daylight. Tomorrow's meeting with the Ambassador was already arranged. Meanwhile, he nosed about the place. The street with its plane trees, the green gate with its two rotten planks, already seemed familiar to him. He had explored the boundaries of the garden and found a place where the wall could be climbed without too much trouble. He had gone over there and pushed his way far enough through the tangled bushes to get a good look at the house. There were two lights burning on the first floor. As he watched, one of the lights went out.

Vogel peered through the mesh of branches at the other light. The curtains were drawn so that he could see nothing of the room, but he knew that Morrell must be in there. Vogel gave a secret smile. He had tracked these experts to their lair, and they did not know it. The thought gave him pleasure. Let them rest easy for a while. The smile left Vogel's face. He had a personal score to settle with these people. They had killed one of his men. No, it was more than that, as he could admit in the privacy of his heart. More than that: they had killed his remembrancer, the whisperer in his ear. He felt it as a threat against himself. Vogel turned away from the thought. It was too uncomfortable, too extravagant for him.

A little later, sitting in his car, Vogel's mood had become more practical. He was wondering how they could go about rescuing Morrell. There was no hope of simply breaking in and taking him. It was going to call for stratagems : nets and traps. That was all right by Vogel.

14

On the President's desk in the Oval Office of the White House there lay a sheet of paper. Beside it was the envelope the President had opened with his own hand about an hour before. The President stared thoughtfully at the paper, then at his assistant, George Hagan. He tapped the paper with a fore-finger. The President had the air of a man waiting for inspiration.

Hagan, the man on the other side of the desk, had been a friend of the President's since his days at Harvard. He had gone on to make a name for himself as a historian and it had given the President peculiar satisfaction to enlist him as his chief aide. He valued Hagan's opinions and felt he knew enough about him to trust him, but there had been something else in the appointment of Hagan, a sly mischievous amuse-ment the President had gained from bringing this old friend and distinguished historian face to face with the realities of government.

Hagan, for his part, had adapted fast. His thinking had shed its impartiality and become essentially tribal. He was now an earnest and determined taker of sides, very proud of his position as Assistant to the President and becoming more ambitious on his own account, attracted by power and the rivalries of office. What was written on the sheet of paper he saw, among other things, as an opportunity. It gave him the chance to use his influence in order to strike at an opponent whose policies he disliked and whose personal aggrandizement irked him – but he knew he must tread carefully.

The two men stared at the sheet of typewritten paper, the President gaunt and brooding, Hagan round-faced and bespectacled. They looked quite ordinary, these two men in their business suits, but they wielded immense power and they knew it.

The President lifted his eyes from the desk. 'You can't help but be galled,' he remarked. His voice had not changed, it remained the usual friendly drawl. 'It's like somebody spitting in your face. My first reaction is to want to sock them one. Do you feel the temptation, George?'

'Oh, I feel it, Mr President, of course I feel it, but on the other hand . . .'

'Sure. I know. We can't afford these simple responses. They have him, George.' He paused. 'I wonder how the hell they got on to Morrell? Did some academic talk?' He smiled wryly at Hagan. 'One thing about the intellectual Establishment – they're always talking. They are very verbal types.'

'Certainly a leak somewhere,' said Hagan. He kept his voice neutral, as befitted a former academic.

'Anyway, the fact remains they've got him. You did check on Morrell's S. rating?' The President knew the answer already but felt the question was worth another airing. It led them on towards certain speculations he knew both of them were privately making.

'Yes. I checked. The Pentagon confirms. At this moment, Morrell is *supremely* important to our security,' Hagan declared, speaking with slow, vehement emphasis.

'At this moment,' echoed the President. 'And these bastards give us five days! Not very generous, George. We lack elbow room.'

'Five days –' Hagan ran his tongue round his lips – 'of which twelve hours are gone already.'

'But would they do it, George? Would they really do it?

Or are they bluffing?'

'They've already killed one man.'

The President gave Hagan a piercing glance, then looked away. 'The other thing,' he drawled, 'would be an extensive demolition job.'

Hagan saw his advantage. 'But we do *need* Morrell,' he urged. 'We happen to need him in a quite unique way.'

'Yes, George. Whereas in Government nobody is irreplaceable. One of the great lessons of politics.' His voice faded. He sat, smiling, waiting.

Hagan cleared his throat. He would have preferred the initiative to come from the President but he saw that, though the President might do the prompting, it was he who would have to make the actual suggestion. 'Looked at in one way,' he began, 'the demands these terrorists are making might be seen as . . . apposite.' He gave a nervous snort of laughter.

'Apposite?' The President's tone was imponderable.

'I mean, they might have come at a good time for us. Lots of people would welcome a change. I won't hide it from you, Mr President, that a great many influential party workers, not to mention members of the general public, are of the opinion that the Secretary . . .'

'So you think we should accede to their demands right away?'

'There is,' said Hagan, plunging in, 'such a thing as a man becoming a political liability. Wouldn't you agree? If he hurts the Party . . .' Hagan shrugged. 'You have the future to think of, Mr President.' He meant not only the future of the Party but also the chance of another term in office for the President, and not least he meant his own future. Hagan had no wish to go back to being a historian now he had tasted the excitements of the West Wing.

'That's true,' said the President, managing to sound as though the idea were new to him. 'But opinion in these matters is never easy to gauge, George. It's a tricky business. Besides,' he went on, 'there is something in me that abhors the idea of knuckling under. I just hate to see a gang of hoodlums putting the squeeze on the United States Government. I certainly don't appreciate their fingers at *my* throat, I can tell you.' He gave a grimace. 'OK. Let's just suppose the course of action these terrorists are trying to force on us is one which we might – I only say *might* – have been thinking about anyway. Even then, George, I prefer to make my own decisions. Nobody enjoys being steam-rollered.'

'Well, of course not,' said Hagan, aware that he might have gone too fast. If his opinions were not taken up, they became dangerous to him. 'All the same,' he added, lamely, 'what else can we do?'

The President seemed to understand Hagan's uneasiness. He gave him an encouraging smile. 'What I'm inclined to do, George, is take a calculated risk. That'll be my first move. As you pointed out just now, we have four days at our disposal. In my judgement, we must devote a couple of those days to the possibility of freeing Morrell.' He held up a hand for silence. 'Don't worry, George,' he said, 'just think about this. So far as the terrorists are concerned, we have one great advantage over them. We know where they are, but *they* don't know that we know. They think they've got away with it. They must be feeling pretty good. Jumpy, of course, waiting for some sign from us, but all the same they won't be expecting trouble. Not at their end. They think they're in the clear. Now, suppose we *gave* them some trouble. If you have an advantage, George, you should always try to make use of it.'

'How?' asked Hagan grudgingly.

'I'm not sure how. That decision has got to be left to the man on the spot. But I think we should instruct our people to try to get Morrell out within the next couple of days. Of course, the thing may not be feasible – I leave that to the judgement of the officer in charge. But I shall urge it, George, I shall urge it.'

'It means us taking one hell of a risk. We could lose Morrell.'

'Not so big a risk, when you think about it. They aren't going to kill Morrell, or only as a last resort. Suppose the

77

attempt fails and they realize their true position? They certainly won't want to kill him *then*. What have they got without Morrell? Not a damn thing. They won't throw away their ace. They'd be finished if they did. They know that. It's a calculated risk, George. Like most of politics.'

Hagan sighed. 'And if the attempt fails?'

'Then,' said the President, 'would be the moment to take up our other alternative. Reluctantly,' he added, his voice unfathomable. 'It could be a tricky operation, and time will be short, so we'd better go straight ahead and make our dispositions in that respect, too.' The President smiled. 'There will be a file, George. Perhaps you could arrange to have it on my desk.'

'A file?' said Hagan, startled. 'On *him*?'

'Certainly, George. They have a file on us all.'

'Ah,' said Hagan. He was a little uncomfortable with the idea at first, but then he thought of the uses to which this file might be put, and his spirits rose again.

15

Arthur Morrell could not get any sleep that first night. He sat in the armchair, very much aware of the eyes of the man the others called Moishe resting on him. Morrell was also very much aware of the presence of Moishe's gun. He carried the knowledge of it like a heavy weight through the long hours of darkness. The gun in Moishe's hand was the same gun that had killed Garen. It could just as easily kill him. Morrell was under no illusions on that score. He found his situation almost incredible and yet he was utterly persuaded of its truth. The scene might be shocking to him but it was in no way unreal. He did not believe he was caught up in a bad dream.

He tried to hold his thoughts together, staring down at the carpet, his eyes following the pattern of the dusty red roses. His eyes traced the outline of the flowers again and again and his thoughts went round and round likewise. Why were they holding him? What did they hope to gain? They had spoken of terms, messages to the White House, impossible things. But they had not told him what it was they wanted. And if the terms were not met? Arthur Morrell could guess. They would shoot him. He winced, imagining the final moment when the gun pointed at him. How would they do it? He remembered reading how the KGB killed their victims: they walked them down a corridor, the executioner following the condemned man, and when the time came, the man was shot without warning, right in the base of the skull. Morrell's mind dwelt on that roaring moment, the furious entry of the bullet. How long would it take? It might look instantaneous, but who knew what happened? Who knew how long such an instant lasted for the victim? To hold eternity in one's hand. The line of verse took on a new sinister meaning to Morrell. He cast a stealthy look at the gun. Eternity in one's hand. Would they really shoot him in cold blood? After Garen he could not doubt it, and yet he had sensed a fragility about their ruthlessness, at least with the younger two. The man across from him was the most dangerous, the one they called Moishe. Morrell frowned. Moishe? Surely that was a Jewish name? What would Jewish terrorists be doing with him? Most likely the name was false, he decided, meant to deceive him. The man did not even look like a Jew: big, fair-haired, tanned by the sun. Who were they? he asked himself. They spoke English well. Who were they?

Twice in the course of the night he heard Moishe clear his throat as if he were about to make some remark, but if so he must have thought better of the idea. It was Arthur Morrell who spoke first. Towards morning, he had to confess a need for the toilet.

Moishe led him out of the room and along a landing. The floorboards were bare, unpolished, noisy underfoot. The walls of the landing were a dingy green. The toilet itself was an antique; a tank of embossed iron, a cracked bowl, a rusty chain to pull.

'Leave the door open,' said Moishe, pointing the gun. Then he added, 'Sorry about that.' Morrell found this blend of menace and courtesy unnerving.

Later the girl, Rachel, cooked breakfast and his kidnappers asked him to join them at table. Morrell found it hard to swallow. He had no appetite. The other three did not talk much, neither to him nor among themselves. His presence seemed to embarrass them, but now and then, in an awkward way, they tried to put him at his ease. Once, when he caught Rachel's eye, she even smiled at him. She was a pretty girl, slight, with an oval face and dark lustrous melancholy eyes. She was wearing her hair loose this morning and it fell over her shoulders. It was curious, thought Morrell, but he had remembered her as a blonde. Now her hair was black. He realized she must have been wearing a wig the night before. Rachel's smile led Morrell to think of Judith. If everything had gone right, he would be back with Judith by now. They would be together in her flat, sitting at the table by the window, watching the sun strike along the river, turning its waters into molten gold. There would be good coffee to drink, not the muddy tea these people gave him, and Judith would have cooked his favourite breakfast, pancakes with syrup. Morrell felt a desperate pang of loss. He might never be with Judith again. Nobody would worry about him yet; not Judith, not his colleagues, not his wife. They would just assume he had been delayed. That was nothing unusual. By the time they began to ask questions, it could all be over. He bowed his head again, a man in mourning for himself.

'There's toast and marmalade,' came Rachel's shy voice. 'Please help yourself.' She sounded sorry to see him so weighed down.

Morrell felt absurdly grateful for her sympathy, but this feeling did not last. It changed almost at once into calculation.

He began wondering whether he might somehow enlist Rachel's sympathy and turn it to his own advantage. At the thought, his tiredness fell away. He took Rachel up on her offer and when she passed him the toast, he found a smile for her that had done him good service with women in the past. Rachel seemed a little flustered. At least, she dropped her eyes.

Morrell had learned by now that the terrorists possessed a radio, but they kept it in the next room and would not let him listen. Every hour, one of the men would go and turn the radio on. David went and did so now. Morrell could hear the low mumble of the announcer's voice, but it was impossible to make sense of the bulletins. He could only pick out the odd word here and there. He strained to catch his own name but did not hear it, and was left wondering what was going on in the world outside this room. Were any plans being made to help him? Maybe, right at this moment, somebody out there was pondering on the terms which could bring about his release. The idea was alarming to Morrell and he shied quickly away from it.

He glanced towards the window but it told him nothing. Between the iron bars Morrell could see nothing more than the tops of some grimy evergreen shrubs and, farther away, a yellow chimney-pot and the dormer window of an attic. Dirty rags of cloud were moving across the sky. It looked as if it might be going to rain. Morrell was seized by a great longing to look out of the window. This room, with its shabby arm-chairs and bare walls, had only the most provisional existence. It was like some drab station waiting-room, a place to drag out the time between trains – except that, for him, this might be the terminus. He might never move on from here.

Morrell felt cowed, like an animal shut in a strange cage. He was tormented by a desire to walk over to the window and look outside but he did not dare do anything about it. He wondered why the terrorists had not bothered to hide their faces from him. Should he read an ominous meaning into that? All the same, it was not easy to keep in mind that these three young people were killers. Most of the time they seemed friendly. Morrell looked over to the window again. It beckoned him.

They left the breakfast table while David was still out of the room. Morrell watched Rachel clearing away the dirty plates. She took them out of the room and he heard her foot-steps going downstairs. The kitchen must be on the floor below.

'Would you have any objection if I stretched my legs?' asked Morrell.

Moishe was leaning against the back of a chair, lighting a cigarette. 'Hm?' he said vaguely. 'What?'

'Stretch my legs. Take a bit of exercise.'

'Help yourself.'

Morrell began to walk up and down between the table and the wall.

Moishe yawned. 'These late nights,' he said. 'I really must stop these late nights.'

Morrell managed a nervous snicker. It was not really laughter, but it stood in for laughter. There was a hint of friendliness in Moishe's voice, the suggestion of a shared joke. Morrell was aware of the need to cultivate any feeling of that sort between them. And then, suddenly:

'Keep away from the window!'

Morrell had been veering slowly across the room. Now he turned as if in surprise, saw the narrow line of the man's mouth, the cold eyes, the gun. 'I'm sorry,' he muttered, 'I didn't realize.' He altered course but he did not stop walking. He did not want to give Moishe the impression that he was offended.

'Keep clear of it, that's all.'

'Just as you say.'

Moishe nodded. 'I do say.'

Morrell went on pacing up and down.

'You smoke?' asked Moishe, as if to make amends.

Morrell came to a halt. His eyes crinkled in an anxious smile. 'Sometimes. Not often. My chest . . .'

'Do you want a cigarette?'

'May I?' Morrell thought it wise to accept. He tried a joke. 'The prisoner's last request?'

'Oh, I hope not.' Moishe smiled. 'I shouldn't think so.'

Morrell was encouraged. 'What are you keeping me here for?' he asked in a humble voice.

'Ah,' said Moishe. He grinned and tapped the side of his nose with a brown forefinger. 'A liddle matter of business.'

'Business?'

'Let's call it an exchange of merchandise.'

'It seems so strange. I mean, I'm not an important man.'

Moishe shook his head. 'Very precious.'

Morrell kept trying. 'I have some small reputation in the scientific world, but surely that's not enough . . .' Morrell let his voice fade. There came into his mind the remark he had made to the Ambassador when he was objecting to Garen. 'A very modest degree of fame.' How far away it seemed, that interview in the sumptuously-furnished office. Morrell felt it had taken place in a different country, another life. How long ago had it been? Not more than two days.

Moishe said: 'We think you're very valuable.'

'Good Lord,' exclaimed Morrell. He managed to sound baffled. 'You astonish me. You really do.' He refused to contemplate the truth. At that moment he desperately wanted to believe that he was still the man he used to be, the scientist, devoted to research. He thrust the military project out of his mind and almost managed to convince himself that it did not exist. His bewilderment was hardly feigned at all. 'You know what,' he said. 'I think you must have got hold of the wrong person.' As he spoke, he became aware of David standing in the doorway. 'Are you sure you know who I am?'

'Certainly we know who you are,' said Moishe. 'You are Arturo Morello, President Elect of the Annamese Republic. Don't bother to deny it.'

'But that's not true,' cried Morrell. 'Oh no! That's not true.' Hope exploded in him like a bomb.

'How do you mean, it's not true?' Moishe spread his hands. His face wore a look of astonishment.

83

'It's just not true. My name is Morrell. Professor Arthur Morrell. I'm a scientist.'

Moishe gave a frown. 'What do you think of that, David? He says his name is Arthur Morrell.'

'An alias. It has to be an alias.'

'No, no. I really am Professor Arthur Morrell . . . You can check . . . I assure you, gentlemen . . .'

'Then it looks as if we have made a terrible blunder,' declared Moishe gravely.

For a moment Morrell was so distraught, so blinded by the promise of freedom, that he believed them. His frame was shaken by a huge, dry sob. Then he saw they were laughing at him and his thoughts slowly cleared. He was driven back into reality, and when he arrived there, they were still laughing. Morrell nodded at them; he even gave a pained smile. 'All right,' he said. 'So now you've had your joke.'

'Really,' said David, 'you mustn't go playing the innocent with us.'

'And don't rate yourself so low,' said Moishe. 'Haven't you heard? Morrell has become a collector's piece. And we've collected.'

Morrell stood between them, head hung down, every line of his body expressing disappointment. He was wondering how they could have got their information. So few people knew. He felt threatened by their certainty.

'Shit!' said Moishe, after a little while. 'I can't bear to see you so hangdog, Professor. Do you play chess?'

Morrell nodded.

'Sit down to table. We'll have a game.'

Moishe took a chess-set out of the table drawer and indicated to Morrell that he should set up the pieces. He put the gun away in his coat pocket and they began to play. Morrell was good at chess and he found to his surprise that the disappointment left in him by the cruel joke had sharpened his brain. He was thinking more clearly now than at any time since his capture. He won the first game without trouble, taking a small, sharp pleasure in the victory that he was careful not to show. 'Ah well,' said Moishe. 'At least it helps to pass the time,' but after his fourth defeat in a row, Moishe felt the need to restore the situation. 'One more,' he said. They began to play the fifth game but when Morrell threatened to break through Moishe's defences yet again, Moishe drew the ·38 from his pocket and pointed it at his opponent.

'Check!' he said.

'Ah,' said Morrell. 'I'm in a hopeless position. I resign, of course.'

They both laughed. It was another joke of a black sort, but Morrell was aware of it as more than that. It gave back to Moishe that fraction of his authority which had been taken from him by his run of defeats.

'The thing is,' said Moishe, 'I'm tired.' He gave a smile of mock apology. 'Don't you want to get some sleep, Professor?'

Morrell shook his head.

'You should have played my father,' said Moishe. 'He would have given you a good game.'

'Your father?' Morrell looked at him enquiringly.

'No chance of a contest now,' said Moishe. 'He's dead.'

The word tolled like a knell in Morrell's heart. 'I'm sorry,' he said, his voice small and dry.

Moishe turned away. He left Morrell with David and went and lay down in the bedroom. He let his thoughts remain on his father. It was always an encouragement to Moishe to think of his father. 'Jacob Hartmann,' murmured Moishe, remembering the grave in the Galilean hills, 'you were quite a man.' It had been no easy thing his father had done. There had been some astonishment in Leeds, so his father had told him, smiling mischievously, considerable surprise when he announced his plans. Moishe had been eleven then. He could still call to mind the hangar-like warehouse with the name painted in big red letters over the door: 'J. Hartmann: Tyre Specialist.' His father was already, at that time, well past forty, firmly established in business, and about the last person the Jewish community in Leeds would have expected to embark on any rash schemes. Yet, a year after his wife's death, he announced he would sell up and go to Israel, taking his three children with him. So all right, but the man would not be setting up in business there, he would be entering a kibbutz, and no ordinary kibbutz, either, but one of the most austerely religious type. It seemed out of keeping. The idea worried people, not least Jacob's sister, Leah, David's mother, who had travelled all the way from Brighton to Leeds to tell her brother that she thought the loss of his wife had affected his brain. Leah made it clear she was not alone in her opinion. Friends and neighbours had told her they thought they might see Jacob Hartmann back in Leeds again before the year was out.

Well, he had proved them all wrong, thought Moishe with a fond smile. Jacob Hartmann had stayed at the kibbutz for the rest of his life. He declared himself a happy man, never happier, so he told Moishe, than when he handed over the money from the sale of his business to the communal chest. Money, he used to say, was too harsh a master for a man to serve all his life. His children had grown up with him on the kibbutz, but now Jacob Hartmann was dead and so was Moishe's brother, Simon. Only Emmie was left, his sister Emmie with her plump complacent husband and her smart apartment in Tel Aviv. Moishe did not want to think about Emmie. She might as well have never left Leeds. She had certainly gone back there in her soul. He did not want to think of the desperate months he had endured in Emmie's flat, after the Bureau retired him. His thoughts went back to his father and to Simon. The son had perished before the father, slaughtered on the Metulla road. It was Simon's death which had first driven the iron into Moishe's soul. The murder of Simon had given rise in Moishe to a tough, durable hatred – which perhaps was why the Bureau had approached him. Hatred was an advantage in the trade they wanted him to ply. Ten years later they turned him off, bloody-handed and sick at heart, offering him their thanks and the impossible advice that he should forget political issues and settle down to life in the ordinary world.

86

Moishe's eyes closed.

Morrell felt David staring at him curiously. He looked as if he would have liked to talk. The two of them were not alone. Rachel was about now. She must have finished the washing-up. Morrell realized that Rachel was never very far from David if she could help it. She moved about the room, doing her best to tidy it. He let his eyes rest on her now and then, as if by chance. It was natural she should attract his attention. After all, she was the only beautiful thing in sight. He would have smiled at her again, if he had dared, but he did not want to risk antagonizing the young man beside him.

Morrell began to wonder again if he would ever get out of this awful room. As if in answer, a memory came to him and he closed his eyes so as to hold on to it. He was lying among tall grasses. He knew the place, a clearing among the woods in Vermont. It was early summer, the air alive with insects. Scents were drifting on the breeze. There was the sweetness of mown grass, the tang of woodsmoke, the quick, subtle perfume of crushed herbs. He lay there, eyes shut, the sun warming his face, utterly at peace, with Judith beside him. The memory was so poignant that he could have cried out, and yet it was a mirage, a lie. He had never been there, at least not with Judith. What had come back to him was an afternoon from long ago, from a time when he was young and filled with the overwhelming sense of promise which comes with young love.

The woman lying beside him had not been Judith Glass. It was a girl he had once worshipped but whose name he now scarcely remembered. 'Janet,' he told himself, 'Janet Drummond.' That had been a wonderful moment, when they lay in the clearing, content, filled with a tenderness for each other so strong it seemed enough to change the world. Less happy moments had followed. Janet Drummond had left him in the end. She had gone quite suddenly and the wound in his self-esteem had opened again, too deep ever to heal over. He had heard later that she married a vet, a man called Smith who took her to live in Iowa. Well, that was all long ago, and her name performed no magic for Morrell now. Janet Smith, née Drummond, meant nothing : what still lived was that moment in the Vermont glade. It survived miraculously, set free from time. Yet now, in Morrell's memory, it seemed as if it were Judith who lay beside him, and he was no longer the scientist old enough to be her father, the man with the bald spot and the grey hair. He and Judith were both young, with the world ahead of them. There was a bright beckoning future, the promise of happiness. It could still happen, he told himself. If he came out of this alive, he would *make* it happen. And then he remembered his wife with her bitter virtue, his children grown up and almost turned to strangers, the crow's-feet round his eyes, the long list of women he had thought he loved. All the same, it could happen, he insisted. With Judith, it could still happen. That was the pledge he had been given. He had only to keep himself alive and this time the future would be different. Everything would come right. Morrell was certain of it. He vowed to do all in his power to stay alive.

If the young man called David wanted to ask questions about micro-biology, as he began to do now, very well, Morrell would do his best to answer them. He would be obliging. He would take every chance that offered of consolidating his hold on life. Morrell settled into his most affable conversational style, reminding himself how much harder it must be to shoot a man with whom you have been in friendly discussion. He answered questions on the uses of phages in gene transfer and the hopes of correcting replication mechanisms where the genetic information was defective. David seemed shrewd and well informed. Clearly, he had a training in the subject.

'So far,' said Morrell, 'my work has concentrated on micro-organisms, but the possibilities for controlled gene-expression in human beings are becoming clear.' He did not choose to admit how far such research had gone already, nor the sinister directions in which he had steered it at the request of Government. As he talked, Morrell could almost imagine himself back at University, holding forth to some promising student. It was like a taste of bygone innocence.

After some time Morrell said mildly, 'You've been asking me a lot of questions. May I ask you a question now?'

'Go on,' said David.

'What use,' said Morrell, appealing not only to David but to Rachel as well, 'what possible use to you is a man like myself?' He tried to strike a note of mild reproach.

David's manner changed abruptly. His eyes glittered. The words came quickly off his tongue. 'A great deal of use. I think you know that.'

Morrell shook his head. He had no need to lie. He raised his handsome face to stare, first at David, then at Rachel, and his blue eyes were clear and candid. It was a relief to be able to speak honestly. 'I haven't the least idea. I don't know why you're holding me nor what you mean to do. I'm baffled.'

'You don't *have* to know,' said David. 'Maybe it's not in your interest to know.'

'All right. Why me? Why Arthur Morrell?'

'Let's say, Professor, that you've become the first victim of your own success.'

'That doesn't make much sense, I'm afraid.'

'Think about it, Professor. You'll find it does. We happen to know about certain aspects of your work, aspects that have not been made public. You were tempted by the devil, weren't you, Professor? And you gave way. You're in no position to protest your virtue.'

'And you?' said Morrell breathlessly.

'Meaning?'

'You've killed one person already,' said Morrell, his voice shrinking to a whisper.

'One person!' said David. 'One person! You aren't so modest, are you? You only plan to kill off half the world! That's all! Oh, you're pleasant enough as a man, and you're a clever scientist, but you've chosen to make a monster of yourself. That's why we need you — because you've turned yourself into a monster. We don't want the scientist, we want the monster. It's the monster that the State loves and cherishes.' David fixed him with accusing eyes. 'A monster that has agreed to lay a curse upon the seed of man!'

'No! No!' said Morrell. Even in his anguish the Biblical extravagance of the words struck him. He felt a desperate need to turn the conversation elsewhere, escape his sense of guilt, make a call somehow on their sympathy. 'Shall I die?' he murmured. 'Would you shoot me?'

There was a silence broken only by the sharp intake of Rachel's breath.

'I mean,' said Morrell, 'if you don't get what you want. Would you kill me then?'

David jumped to his feet and stood there, shaking. He opened his mouth but nothing came out.

'I should like to know,' Morrell persisted. 'It would be as well to prepare myself.'

'I don't think you'll get hurt,' said David, his voice slurring with passion. He was flushed, hot-eyed. 'But your future doesn't rest with us.'

'Who does it rest with, then?'

'With certain other powerful monsters. They're the ones who'll make the choice on you, Professor. It's as simple as that.'

'Nothing is simple,' said Morrell. 'I've learnt that much in my life.'

'Damn you!' cried David. 'Don't bullshit me.'

But Morrell could hear the tension in his voice, the lack of certainty. He felt he had gained some ground by this dangerous conversation. He was becoming less of an object to them, more of a man. They were beginning to be entangled in each other's pain. 'I'm sorry,' he said.

'And don't be sorry!' yelled David. 'Cut out the humility! It doesn't sound too well, coming from a man like you.' He sounded wounded, hurt by his own anger. Rachel went across to him and touched his arm. 'David,' she said. 'It's all right.' Her eyes sought out Morrell. She looked as if she would have liked to apologize.

David shook himself free. 'I'll tell you what is simple,

Professor,' he said. 'A bullet is simple. That's one thing *I've* learnt lately.' He thrust the gun in Morrell's face, the muzzle close to his forehead.

'For God's sake!' cried Rachel, pulling his arm away. 'Don't say such things, David. Don't talk like that.'

'Oh, but we must,' said David, breathing hard. 'From now on we must.'

Morrell gave a shuddering sigh. Despite his fear and the calculations to which it drove him incessantly, he found room in his heart for a moment's pity, seeing the anguish of these two young people who had become his gaolers. He recognized that they, like him, were driven towards ends which in a different world they would never have chosen. But, unlike him, they were so young.

'You know,' he heard himself say mildly, 'I've got a couple of children of my own. A girl and a boy. They're about the same age as you two.'

'Stop that!' shouted David, his eyes staring. 'Don't give us that sort of stuff.' He shook his fist at Morrell. 'I don't want to hear any more from you. Understand that, Morrell? From now on I want to hear nothing about your life. Nothing about your work. Nothing about your family. Nothing about what goes on in your head. I want to know nothing of you whatsoever. Just sit in that chair and keep your mouth shut.'

'Hey,' said Moishe, appearing in the doorway. 'What's all the noise? You woke me up.'

David stared out of the window. He had the air of a guilty child.

'Stay cool,' said Moishe, smiling. 'Excitement is bad for the digestion.'

David spun round on him. 'I'm sorry,' he said, in a bitter voice. 'Blame it on the ghetto blood. It's coming out in me again, cousin.'

Moishe refused to take offence. 'Listen,' he said. 'The lawyer who gets his feelings mixed up with those of his client, that man is a fool. The same goes for a doctor and his patient. And we . . . well, we can't afford to get ourselves mixed up with him.' He pointed to Morrell.

David went on staring out of the window.

Moishe took him by the shoulders. 'Think what we're doing, David,' he said. 'Think of the stakes. We can't afford to give way to our emotions. Not about him. Not even about ourselves. In this game we're all expendable, but we don't just go and *blow* it!'

David nodded. He gave a wry smile. 'I'm sorry,' he said, blinking fast. 'I shouldn't have got so uptight.'

'It's reaction,' said Moishe. 'That's all. Last night you were good. You were very, very good last night, David. The way you went in there – that was great! It took real nerve. Now comes the reaction. We all get it.'

Moishe stood back from David. 'You know,' he said, 'I've always felt your namesake must have been a very emotional guy. He was an artist, a musician. A man of feeling. He wasn't only into the harping and the singing, it was dancing with him, too. He was even dancing before the Lord – Still, he didn't manage things so badly.'

The two men looked at each other and began to grin.

'Come on,' said Moishe, taking David's arm and leading him towards the bedroom. 'We have some business to talk over. You, too, Rachel. You'd better be in on this.'

Rachel threw Morrell a startled glance before she followed them.

Morrell found himself alone. He wondered anxiously what they were talking about in the next room. The door was open but they kept their voices down and he could not make out what they were saying. Just once he heard Rachel cry, 'Must he?' This was followed by an undistinguishable murmur of male voices, and though he strained his ears he could not pick up any more words. Must he? thought Morrell. Must he what? He stared uneasily around the room. Very slowly he eased himself up out of the chair. If he could reach the door . . . It was not far away, a matter of twelve feet. He told himself he ought to run. His best plan was to make a dash for it. Beyond the door lay the corridor, the stairs, the road to freedom. But Morrell did not feel able to run. His heart seemed to have come loose, it was lurching about in his chest like a machine that has broken free of its housings. He decided he would run, all the same, but he could not persuade his muscles to obey. Running was so . . . unambiguous. He feared it might provoke an equally unambiguous response. Better to sidle forward, to edge excruciatingly over towards the door. It was the only way he could manage to move at all. His face was screwed up, like the face of a man anticipating a blow.

'What do you think you're doing, Professor?'

Morrell twisted round to see Moishe in the doorway of the bedroom, a gun in his hand.

'Lavatory,' he said thickly. 'Have to go.'

'Sit down a while,' said Moishe, cheerful and unconvinced. 'Tie a knot in it, Professor. And just remember.'

'Remember? Remember what?'

'Remember the chauffeur!'

Hearing these words, Morrell was quick to get back to his seat. He found it a relief to be free of the burden of trying to escape.

16

Vogel was reasonably happy with the dispositions he had made. The house was under observation, the garden bugged, he had men on the move in the neighbourhood. The place was sealed up tight as a cork in a bottle. On the other hand, he was far less happy with the orders he had been sent. Vogel reckoned he had been asked to perform the near-impossible. What's more, he had been asked to perform it within the next forty-eight hours – and for reasons Washington had not seen fit to divulge. Great!

The support of the British SIS had been sought. It was

not just a matter of courtesy. Facilities might be needed beyond the scope of any Service not operating on its home territory. All this had meant so far to Vogel was that he found himself saddled with a liaison officer from British Intelligence, a man not falling under his direct command, which was something else he could have done without. However, SIS had been co-operative. At his request, they issued instructions to local police and the CID that they should ignore the operation unless they were specifically called in. That was not going to happen.

Vogel did not find himself exactly enraptured by the man who turned up on behalf of British Intelligence, either. In the course of his job, Vogel had become acquainted at one time or another with various members of the SIS, but Austen Roper was not an officer they had chosen to let him meet before. Roper was a man of slender build, though his shoulders were surprisingly broad. He was taller than Vogel, and appeared to be about the same age. He had a narrow face with a hard regularity about the features and a blue polished chin. Vogel conceded that the man was handsome in a shadowy, twilit way. Roper's skin was very pale, stretched tight across his cheekbones, and under the grey eyes there were purple bruises. He had the slightly singed, wasted look of a man who keeps himself in rigorous training, but though his belly was flat and his features lean, he did not strike Vogel as somebody much given to outdoor pursuits. There was no sunlight in his face. It suggested nights spent among the steam of the Turkish bath, hours on the masseur's bench, lecherous grapplings in shoddy rooms. He was fit, but his body lacked the repose of an athlete. There was a hungry, watchful quality about it. Roper had the air of a night creature, a prowler among dark streets, a man who maintained himself against the odds. As for his get-up, Vogel found that deplorable.

By the time Roper arrived, Vogel had installed himself in his operational headquarters – the attic room of the house across the road from where the terrorists were lurking. Vogel had rented the attic because it was the only place that overlooked the terrorists' hide-out. It hadn't been hard to get the room. When he saw the amount of money offered, the Indian landlord had ordered a prompt evacuation of the attic by the old uncle he had been harbouring there.

The landlord was a plump man with wet, brown eyes that shone like sucked toffees. He had a pouting mouth much given to ingratiating smiles. Vogel had watched the movement of the lips with slight distaste while the Indian explained to him in voluble terms that his uncle would be found other quarters and that, for his own part, he could be relied upon to do everything possible to promote the comfort and convenience of his new tenant. The Indian's manner was tenderly obsequious, softened by money and fear.

'All I want is no talk,' said Vogel. 'Keep your own counsel, Mr Patel. That's all I ask of you.'

'Of course. Not a word, sir. I understand.' Patel rubbed his hands together nervously. Vogel did not foresee any trouble from him. He guessed Patel had secrets of his own to protect, matters to do with the Inland Revenue, that sort of thing.

'This is official business,' said Vogel, knowing the phrase would weigh heavily with the landlord. 'But it doesn't concern you directly, Mr Patel. I want you just to carry on as usual.'

'All will be as absolutely normal, sir. I am assuring you of that.' The Indian's forehead showed a faint haze of sweat.

'There are going to be visitors, people coming to see me. I'd like you to ignore them.'

'But of course.' Patel bowed out, clutching the wad of notes in his hand. 'Every person has a fundamental right to privacy,' he declared as he went.

The first visitor was Austen Roper. He and the landlord must have met on the stairs, which, thought Vogel, would have given the Indian some swift food for thought. Roper came in wearing a brown three-quarter-length leather jacket, a lemon polo-necked sweater, tight Levi's, a broad belt with a huge brass buckle and patent high-heeled boots. Vogel found himself staring in disbelief at this apparition. He would never have allowed one of his own people to dress in such outlandish

95

gear, or not without some very good reason. Roper looked as if he might just have come from a gay bar off the King's Road. Vogel might have been able to accept all this as a whimsical sort of cover had it not been for certain other signs he picked up : the way the man had of letting his head tilt, the set of his mouth, and certain inflections of the voice.

Vogel was not pleased. Though his profession had taught him to show no surprise at men's sexual tastes, he had not arrived easily at that position. It had meant suppressing the innate puritanism of his nature. Vogel did not like homosexuals, though he had known several charming and some dangerous exponents of that vice during his career. He remained stubbornly averse to them, despite all the liberal pressures of the age. It was not a matter where he had any choice. He could have argued how he liked, but still the feeling would have remained. It was instinctive, a bias of the flesh. Vogel did not want to interfere with the freedom of perverts to indulge their appetites – let them go to hell their own way – but all the same he could not help feeling that their behaviour was against nature and dishonourable in the deepest of ways. When he thought about such things, which was not often, Vogel could not help but regard sodomy as disgusting. Such an abuse of natural function touched him with confusion and dismay – and this though, in the course of his duties, he had from time to time been obliged to procure pleasures of this kind for other men. Vogel regarded sodomy as one of the entertainments of hell. Satanic vaudeville, disgusting and grotesque, just one part of the evidence which went to prove the fallen state of man. Vogel believed, at a level deeper than reason, in the existence of sin. Despite all contemporary arguments, he had no doubt of the innate evil lurking in men's souls. Indeed, he relied on it often in the course of his job. 'I am the last of the moralists,' Vogel sometimes told himself sardonically. He took a severe pleasure in working through men's weaknesses. He was aware of the ironies of his situation. In fact, he had deliberately sought them out.

When Roper turned up, dressed like a faggot, Vogel thought: I wouldn't take this from any of my own men, but he had checked his annoyance, telling himself that the British nowadays were in decline and absolutely anything could be expected of them. After the loss of their Empire, the British had become spiritually flabby. They deluded themselves, of course, claiming that flabbiness represented an increase in humanity. Vogel did not think so. As Vogel saw it, the British were fast becoming decadent. That was not a matter for surprise to Vogel. Decadence seemed to him the most likely of all human states.

Vogel did not let any of these thoughts show on his face. He hid his disapproval and set out in a neutral voice to give Roper an account of the events in the case so far.

Roper listened closely, fixing Vogel with hard grey enquiring eyes. At the end of Vogel's description he said: 'Well, this is certainly an odd business, Vogel.' He flashed the American a smile. 'You don't mind, by the way, if I call you Vogel?'

'Why should I mind? It's my name.'

'True. But you might wanted to be addressed as "*Mister* Vogel". Or you might cherish a deep yearning to be called "sir".' Roper managed to make both alternatives sound foolish and contemptible. 'Such things have been known.'

' "Vogel" will do.'

'All right. Call me Roper. Well, Vogel, you do have a very weird sort of scene going here. A regular *conundrum* of a scene.'

'What makes you say that . . . Roper?'

'Listen: You tell me there are three people shut up in that house over there.'

'Four.'

'Three *terrorists*.' Roper waved a big, white hand towards the window. Vogel saw with a flicker of distaste that the nails were bitten. 'You tell me these people have kidnapped an American professor, name of Morrell. They're holding him there. But why? You don't tell me that, Vogel. Who the hell *are* these people? You've got nothing to say on that point, either. What terms are they demanding? You haven't been *informed*. Yet you assure me it's all very important, so important that we can't call in the police, and we must make sure the newspapers don't get a hint of the proceedings. It's a completely undercover job. Even to us, by the sound of things.' Roper sighed. 'Very opaque. Very much through a glass darkly, don't you think?'

Vogel was taken aback, almost swamped by this torrent of words. 'I agree,' he said in a grudging voice. 'It is strange.'

'Now, I'm bound to ask myself,' Roper went on, smiling but waspish, 'whether you could be holding something back on yours truly.' He touched his chest with a delicate finger.

'Why should I hold anything back, Roper?'

'An interesting question.' Roper put his head on one side. 'Could it be that you have orders I know nothing about? Orders to restrict information? If that's the position . . .'

'Not so, Roper.'

'Then we have to put your reticence down to something else. Some more *personal* thing, perhaps.'

'Put what down?' asked Vogel irritably.

'Maybe you just can't bring yourself to confide in a fellow like me.' Roper held up a hand. 'No, no, let's pursue that line of thought for a moment. Tell me, Vogel. If I'd worn Donegal tweeds and come striding in with a meerschaum or something clenched between my teeth, would you have been more forthcoming? Just thinking aloud,' he added.

'I don't know what you're driving at, Roper.'

'You don't? Well, well. You surprise me. I'm hinting,' said Roper in patient tones, 'that perhaps you aren't being straight with me, Vogel. What's more, I'm trying to sort out possible reasons why.'

'You've got a nerve, haven't you?' said Vogel, his voice clipped. 'Coming in here and throwing all this at me. You take a lot on yourself.' He was affronted and yet pleased by the abrasive quality of the man. 'I'm levelling with you, Roper. I've given you all I have.'

Roper made a coy, ducking motion of the eyes. 'And so

soon!' he exclaimed, tossing his head.

'For Christ's sake!' Vogel burst out. He told himself to cool down. He was letting himself be needled by this sharp-tongued freak.

Roper became serious again: 'Let me say this, Vogel. From the moment I stepped through the door, I've had to suffer the cold blast of your disapproval. Look at you now, staring at me as if I'd broken wind in your presence and weren't man enough to own up.'

'Very touchy, aren't you, Roper? Very sensitive?'

'Which doesn't mean to say I'm indiscreet. What's the trouble, Vogel? Aren't you happy with me? Would you rather have been assigned some portentous ass in a bowler hat?'

'Since you mention it,' said Vogel with a sour smile at the man's audacity, 'I must admit I'm not overboard about that outfit of yours.'

'No? What do you think is wrong? You're not trying to tell me I lack dress sense?' Roper looked at him with dramatically wounded eyes. 'That would be hard for me to take, Vogel!'

'These games of yours are getting hard for *me* to take,' growled Vogel, though secretly he was beginning to enjoy the confrontation.

'Confess, Vogel. You can't bring yourself to trust a man like me. Who would unburden his secrets to such a frivolous person?' Roper wagged a finger at Vogel. 'I know what it is. You belong to the school of thought which believes that my sort of habits affect the brain. Do terrible things to the nervous system. Turn strong men into weaklings.'

'Don't lean on me, friend. Stop trying to work me over.'

'Tell you what,' said Roper pleasantly. 'You lean on *me*.' He put his elbow down on the table and kept his forearm raised.

Vogel peered at the white creased palm which was being presented to him. 'What's the idea of that?'

Roper looked at him steadily. 'Come on,' he said. 'Floor me. Put me down, General. A man of my sort shouldn't give you

99

too much trouble.'

'What have they sent me?' asked Vogel in a musing voice, but he felt the absurd attraction of the challenge. 'You have to be some kind of a nut, Roper,' he murmured, and yet he found himself solemnly planting his own elbow on the table. 'Me too,' he added, seeing what he was doing. 'The thing is catching!'

The two men locked hands and began to try to push each other's forearms down. Vogel was astonished to find himself involved in this lunatic contest and yet he was not prepared to back out. The two of them struggled for a while, their arms swaying this way and that. Sweat broke out on their foreheads.

Dick Pearson, one of Vogel's junior officers, chose this moment to walk into the room. He was going off duty and had called to make his report. Now he stood bemused, watching his boss, a man known for his austere manner, hand-wrestling a big queer across the office table. The sight set him wondering.

'Don't break off,' urged Roper in a voice that tried to strike a careless note, though it came out through clenched teeth. 'Don't go chickening on me now.'

Vogel nodded. 'Well,' he said to Pearson. 'Anything to report?' He was grunting in his effort to sound casual. 'Any developments?'

Pearson shook his head. 'Nothing as yet, sir.' He stared in fascination at the scene before him.

'OK, Pearson – just take off now, would you, heh?'

The young officer retreated quickly, a baffled look on his face.

After he had left, the match went on for five more minutes without either man being able to gain a decisive advantage.

'What do you reckon?' asked Vogel. 'It looks like a stand-off to me.'

'Acceptable, acceptable. Honour is satisfied.'

They let go of each other.

'What the devil was that in aid of?' asked Vogel, massaging his fingers.

'Try to guess,' Roper smiled. 'I *do* so like a show-down early on in the proceedings. Clears the air, don't you think? Besides,' added Roper, putting on his most insolently camp voice, 'as you can imagine, I take every chance I can of holding hands.'

Vogel gave a snort of laughter. This big bent Englishman intrigued him. He liked the guy's truculence. Vogel had begun to take to Roper in an antagonistic way.

17

Moishe went back into the bedroom. He had left Morrell alone on purpose, knowing what was likely to happen. There was a lesson in it for him.

'The Professor thought he'd take a little walk,' said Moishe cheerfully. 'I wondered if he'd have the nerve to try anything, with us out of the room. It seems he has – but only just. Well, that's worth knowing, I suppose.' He gave David and Rachel an encouraging smile. He knew this must be a difficult moment for them, even though they had talked the matter over and accepted the need for it in the days when everything was still theory. Of course, it was different now. Moishe could see how sad Rachel was at the prospect. For David it was not quite the same. He would not want to leave Rachel but he would have the various consolations of action. Moishe envied him the next phone call to the Ambassador. That would be another heady moment. 'So we're agreed, then?' said Moishe.

David nodded.

'D'you think I could go with him?' Rachel answered her own question. 'No, I can't, can I.'

'It's not for long,' said David.

'Well, *I* can't watch the Professor night and day,' said Moishe, keeping his voice cheerful. 'It needs at least two of us.' Moishe saw the question in Rachel's eyes. 'I think it's better if David goes, rather than me,' he said. 'David is the Englishman. He knows his way around London. That sort of thing.' Moishe did not add that he wouldn't be able to trust David and Rachel with the prisoner if he were away. After the performance he had just witnessed between David and Morrell, it was unthinkable that David should be left in charge here.

'It makes the best sense,' David told Rachel.

'You see,' said Moishe, 'we have to keep on twisting their tails. And it had better not be done from here. You do understand that, Rachel? Besides, somebody has to check the news, keep an eye on the newspapers, arrange the tickets. In fact, we need a man out there, just like we've always said.'

'It won't be for long,' David urged her again.

'But suppose nothing happens?' said Rachel. 'I mean, what if they don't respond? There's been no news. Not a word on the radio . . .'

'You know what that means?' said Moishe. 'It means things are going well for us. Believe me, Rachel. It means the matter is being hushed up. We've heard no mention of Morrell's disappearance. Why not? No reference to a dead man in a certain place. Well, that's good. From our point of view that's very good. You have to realize, such a thing as we've demanded takes a little time, even for the most eminent of statesmen.' Moishe gave a grin.

'Four days at the most,' said David.

'Not as long as that, cousin. They won't leave things to the last minute. They wouldn't want to risk an accident.'

'I wonder what he's thinking now,' said David, suddenly very aware of the pressure that the three of them must be exerting on the man in the Oval Office three thousand miles away.

'He's thinking that we have him by the jugular,' said Moishe. 'He's thinking of all the swear words he knows. Cheer up, Rachel,' he added. 'Right now, we're making a little history.'

Rachel looked from one to another of them. She fought to

put on a brave face. 'Yes,' she said, her eyes shining. 'I'm sure it's going to be all right.'

'I don't know about you lot,' said Moishe, 'but I'm getting hungry.'

Rachel took him up at once. 'I'll go and serve the food. It should be ready now.'

'Good girl,' said Moishe. He wanted to keep her occupied, and he had seen how domesticated a person Rachel was. Even here, in this grubby rat-hole, she took pleasure in keeping house. 'Go with her, David,' he urged. 'I'll stay with our friend.'

He watched them go off, hand-in-hand, then he went back to the living-room and sat down across from Morrell.

'A game of chess, Professor?' he asked in a sly, innocent voice.

'Chess? Sure. Of course.' Morrell was quick to set up the pieces, anxious to make atonement. Even so, after the first few moves had been made, he looked like gaining dominance over the play yet again.

Moishe leant across the board. 'Professor,' he said, 'I thought you said you wanted to take a leak just now?'

'What?' said Morrell, startled. 'Oh, that. It's gone off.' He gave a nervous smile.

The reminder seemed to break Morrell's concentration. At any rate, from then on he started to lose the game.

'What did I tell you?' said Moishe, when he had won. 'I was sure I'd play better, once I'd had a bit of sleep.' He gave Morrell an enigmatic smile.

'Smells good,' said David, sniffing the spicy odours, the fragrance of cooked meat. 'What have you got for us?'

Rachel lifted the lid of the saucepan and a cloud of steam rose towards the ceiling. 'You'll like it. Soon we'll be on to the pre-packed stuff, but this time everything is fresh. I wanted to make something special for tonight.'

David nodded. He understood. 'We have a long time to go,' he said. 'Hours yet.' He stood behind Rachel and kissed the top of her head.

'Now is the moment to eat,' said Rachel briskly. 'We mustn't let it spoil.' Then she turned and buried her face in David's shoulder.

Earlier that day, Rachel had mixed the rice and the grated onion with minced beef and tomato. She had taken the scalded leaves of a white cabbage and wrapped them round the savoury lumps of meat, stitching the leaves with thread so that they would hold firm. Then she had put these leafy parcels into a pan lined with more cabbage leaves and poured over them the special mixture of vinegar and water laced with sugar and sultanas which helped give the dish its character.

She had done all these things in a meticulous, practical way, and yet all of her actions had been meant as an offering to David, an expression of her love, knowing that he would have to go, and that she must not try to stop him. How funny, she thought, to feel the need to declare yourself in terms of sweet-and-sour cabbage, but it was not so strange after all. It was very like human beings to do that sort of thing. She had seen her mother, a woman who was under no obligation ever to enter a kitchen, make just such declarations to her father, not once but many times : 'I love you with *gefillte* fish, my darling. I love you with *matzo kleis*. I love you with lockschen pudding. I love you with cheese blintzes and Purim fritters.' Oh yes, the table no less than the bed was a place for making vows. The table had its ceremonies, in love as in religion. She offered up this dish of sweet-and-sour cabbage to David and he understood the gesture, she could see that by his face. Well, it was nothing so unusual, but she found it moved her very much. 'I mustn't get worked up now,' she told herself. 'I mustn't upset him.' Food was acceptable, tears were not. The sweet and the sour together on the tongue, that was enough.

'Great!' cried David. '*Holishkes.*' His voice rang with undue enthusiasm. He, too, was making his vows.

'And honey cake to follow,' said Rachel. '*Lekach.*' Melting sweetness to follow : a promise on her part, a work of magical intent.

'No doubt about it, Rachel, you're going to be the best wife in Israel.'

'May it come soon,' muttered Rachel under her breath. She began to serve on to the plates. 'David,' she said, 'do you think we could eat by ourselves? Down here?'

'Sure. Why not?'

His face was pale, the skin luminous. Oh, those dark brilliant eyes, the red lips smiling at her, the sumptuous black line of the moustache. Rachel closed her eyes against the sight of him for a moment. 'I could lay up for us here.' Rachel pointed to the kitchen table. The bare wood of the table was bleached the colour of bone. It carried old scars, knife cuts and pot burns.

'No, no,' said David. 'We deserve something a bit better. Your cooking shall have proper respect!' She watched his eager fooling, the way in which he hunched his shoulders and spread his hands. 'I ask you, Rachel : Why *have* the house, if we aren't going to use the house?' She knew how quickly his moods veered, yet this time she understood, and she was grateful for what he was trying to do. She crossed her arms over her breasts and smiled at him.

David went into the room that opened off the kitchen. It had once been the dining-room. There was a serving-hatch that opened in the wall. They could use the room to eat in tonight, he thought, smiling as he remembered the shock he and Rachel had felt when they first saw the hatch. The serving-hatch took the form of a sliding wooden panel. On the kitchen side it had been thought good enough merely to paint the panel the same colour as the wall, but on the other side, where the master and mistress of the house must have taken their meals, the panel had been embellished. A picture had been painted on it, a sombre affair in oils, done in the worst sort of Edwardian style. It showed a Biblical scene – a scene that had astonished them when they had first set eyes on it. Judith and

Holofernes, no less! At first they had laughed, but then they were left wondering. David chose to proclaim the picture a good omen, an augury of their success.

'Of all the stories in the world,' he exclaimed, 'to find this one here! Judith: the woman who saved Israel!'

Rachel nodded, staring hard at the picture.

'And do you realize that Holofernes was the chief minister to Nebuchadnezzar, who at that time happened to be the most powerful ruler in the world? When Judith lopped off his head, she did it in God's name, for the salvation of the people. It's like a sign, Rachel. A sign from Heaven.'

'I wish I liked the picture better,' Rachel had replied. She found it vulgar and dated, but beyond the silliness, the thing had an oddly sinister feel. 'As a painting, it's terrible.'

David agreed. He was puzzled why anyone should want to display such a picture on the wall of their dining-room. He guessed the Biblical story must be a cover, the disguise for some more disreputable private triumph. 'Ignore the technique, think of the subject matter,' he had urged Rachel at the time. Now, standing in front of the painting again, knowing that they held Morrell captive upstairs, he was less than easy at the sight of that agonized head hanging by its black locks from Judith's pale fingers.

He slid the panel open. 'Give me a duster, Rachel.'

She took a tea-towel from the hook on the side of the kitchen cupboard. 'Will this do? It's the nearest thing I've got.'

'Sure.'

Rachel handed the towel through the hatch. Then she took the tray of food upstairs for the others.

David made his way across the dining-room. There were a couple of battered armchairs by the fireplace, and a chaise-longue in which his father might have shown an interest, despite its rotten fabric. This house had never been properly cleared, it had simply been abandoned. David was aware of the weight of past lives, old pretensions, dead hopes. He walked to the mahogany table at the far end of the room. Beyond the table there were french windows, but they let in no light.

Moishe had covered them with heavy drapes.

First, David wiped the dust from the surface of the table, then he took candles from the cupboard and stuck them in jam-jars and lit them. He laid the cutlery and put out a couple of glasses.

By the time Rachel came back, everything was ready. Rachel faced him across the table, her eyes shining in the light of the candles.

'We have hours yet,' he told her tenderly.

She nodded. David said grace and they began to eat.

'Hey,' said David, jumping up from his chair. 'What about the wine? We must have wine with this.'

While he was away, Rachel did not touch a mouthful. She sat very still, her eyes closed, but when David came back, flourishing the bottle, she laughed and clapped her hands. She made her eyes sparkle for him. And when he ate, so did she.

18

'Now tell me,' said Vogel, with the air of a man getting down to business, 'what's your speciality, Roper? In the Department,' he felt the need to add.

Roper saluted this last remark with a wildly rolling eye. 'In the *Department*, it's psychology,' he said. 'And talking of that, Vogel, did nobody ever take you aside and tell you the truth about morbid and irrational loathing?'

'Oh no,' said Vogel. 'You're way out of line there, Roper. You're also pushing your luck.'

'Sure,' said Roper blandly. 'A man's neuroses are his own business.' He paused. 'But now that we've cleared the air, Vogel, perhaps you'd be kind enough to fill in those gaps.'

'The trouble is,' said Vogel, 'that the gaps are real. Believe me, Roper, I'm being kept in the dark about a hell of a lot of stuff myself.'

Roper gave Vogel a hard stare. Then he nodded and walked over to the window. There was a pair of field-glasses lying on the sill. Roper picked them up. 'Mind if I take a look?'

'Help yourself.' Vogel noticed how much deeper and more sombre Roper's voice had suddenly become. The brittle, fractious note had gone. It seemed the man possessed two voices, as different as if they were the property of two separate people. He certainly was a strange guy. While Roper trained the glasses on the house, Vogel stared curiously at his back. At that moment he felt more fascination than disgust for his new associate.

Roper watched the house for quite a time. He felt the need for some respite after his performance earlier. It had not been as enjoyable as he had hoped. It was the old story : pleasures diminished, things lost their edge. Still, it had been necessary. There was the need to establish oneself, and do it on one's own terms. Roper pulled a wry face. That was a bunch of shit, for a start. There had been no reason, no least necessity to invite trouble by coming here looking like a Company tart. He could have dressed quietly, minded his manners and passed himself off as a straight. No need – except that he *had* been a Company tart in his time. He knew the role well. Why not play it again? He had acted the whore for his employers before now – no, not for them, he corrected himself. That was not the truth, either. Basically he had done it for himself. He had used his employers at least as much as they had used him. They had offered him a brew of pleasures headier than any he could find elsewhere. And earlier, when he had flaunted himself to Vogel, it wasn't done out of any allegiance to his condition – that would have been merely ridiculous. It was done to provoke. The performance was meant to assuage yet again, if only for a few moments, the endless hunger Roper felt nowadays for excitement, for outrage. Without that to sustain him, he found it harder and harder to go on.

When he was young, it had been convenient for Roper to believe in nothing much beyond sensation. It ensured that though there was no real meaning in the world, there were still some glittering lodes of pleasure to be mined. He had enjoyed the hurly-burly, the cruising, the rough-trade picked up in tatty bars. Now, when the whirligig stopped and the voices died away – all those voices : spiteful, witty, vicious or sad – very often Roper discovered that the silence was importuning him with a voice of its own. He listened to its whispers and found that what it had to offer was an invitation to oblivion. And, as time passed, the invitation grew more and more pressing.

Roper had always chosen to assume that there were no sure foundations to the world. He had put himself on the high-wire and gone prancing over the abyss. Now it was more often the abyss itself that beckoned. Lying abed in the dark, alone or with some temporary 'friend', Roper found he was being approached by the pimps of nothingness and nowhere. He turned them away, but they always came back. He tried to make his life more wild, more outrageous, to lose himself in action – but they were not impressed. One day, Roper supposed, it would happen . . . one day he would take up their offer, to the astonishment of all who knew him. But not yet. Not quite yet. There was still a part of him that resisted these solicitations. He envisaged his life fizzing desperately away, like a show of fireworks, so many sparkles and flashes and coloured lights thrown up against the patient black gape of the sky.

Roper hunched over the glasses. His eyes had picked out movement on the first floor of the house. He focused the glasses precisely on the young man and woman there. They seemed restless, straying up and down. Beasts in a cage, thought Roper. He knew that feeling. They came to the window and stared out, giving him a clear view of them. Roper was immediately struck by the appearance of the young man. It seemed to him he knew that delicate fawn's head, the oval face, the black hair, the thin line of the moustache. He felt a grudging movement of desire, followed by shame. The young man looked like Hamid, but, of course, that was not possible. Hamid had been dead a long time now.

The young couple at the window kept touching each other. There was a good deal of earnest talk passing between them and all the time they kept up a tender persistent dialogue with their hands, too. Roper gave them his close attention. As always, he was fascinated yet disturbed when confronted with the signs of love. This time his feelings were sharper than usual because the young man looked so very much like Hamid.

Roper had imposed few restrictions on himself but he had not let himself believe in love. Nevertheless, love had come into his life – and his response had been to turn and savage it. After Hamid, he knew he was no longer fit for love. He had abused it beyond forgiveness. This remained true, even though he recognized that love alone might provide some lasting defence against the whispering bawds who came to him in the night.

Roper reminded himself for the thousandth time that Hamid had been an enemy of the British administration – the young fool had got himself mixed up with the terrorists in Aden. But Hamid had also been a generous and trusting boy. Roper had found it laughingly easy to convince Hamid that he was a rich businessman, sympathetic to the aims of the 'freedom fighters'. Roper had accepted Hamid's love, he had even returned it, and yet he still found it in him to betray the young man. He had duped Hamid and sent him to his death, and there had been a wilful devil in his heart that took pleasure in the act. He had not done the job himself. The ambush had been carried out by others, but Roper had supplied the intelligence. It was his duty, of course, but he had also *wanted* it that way. That was the most desolating fact about himself Roper had ever discovered. He had mourned then, not only for Hamid but for the mysterious perversity of his heart. He got drunk and stayed drunk for a week, but even then, what began as grief had ended differently. In his drunkenness he had come under the sway of the same fierce appetites that had found pleasure in Hamid's death. Roper's week of mourning had ended among the heartless lewdness of a male brothel on the waterfront.

Now he looked through the glasses at the young man with the black moustache and reflected that he, too, was going to be destroyed, just as Hamid had been. Why else would the eagles have gathered here? The idea stirred a kind of envious passion in Roper's heart. He turned away from the window, unable to bear the sight of the young couple a moment longer.

'Anything doing?' asked Vogel.

'Yes. Two of them at the window. Young man. Young woman. Dark hair. Dark eyes. What's their nationality? Could they be Arabs?' Roper's voice snagged on the last word.

'We don't know for sure.'

'We don't? Absolutely *steeped* in ignorance, aren't we?' said Roper, his voice rancorous. He batted his eyebrows at Vogel. 'You *are* sure Morrell's still with them? I mean, he hasn't gone off home or anything?'

'He's there, Roper.'

'I've heard of a quiet flap, General, but this is *ridiculous*.'

'Sure, it's strange.'

'In the circumstances, would you mind not being quite so calm about it, Vogel? It doesn't help my confidence any.'

'How many times do I have to say it? I'm not holding out on you.' Vogel smiled, but as always the smile seemed to come from a long way off, as if he had summoned it from another world. 'Tell you what, Roper,' said Vogel, playing the game back to him, 'I'll make a deal with you. I'll do my best to be less calm, if you'll cut out the goddam camping.'

'That's a hard bargain, General!'

'I'd also very much appreciate it if you stopped calling me "General".'

'No fun,' murmured Roper. 'You're just no fun any more.'

'Let's just try and arrive at a little . . . solidity, for Christ's sake.'

Roper sighed. 'I knew it had to come.'

'Listen, Roper. We have big problems, you and I.'

'Don't I just know it, Vogel!'

Vogel kept his temper with difficulty. 'No, you don't. You aren't aware of the full scope of the pressures. And stop looking at me like that. There is another factor . . .'

'Another factor? Here's a little secret coming out!'

'Roper, you really are a provoking sort of bastard.'

'I like to think so.'

'Jesus!' Vogel brought the flat of his hand down hard on the desk. 'Will you *please* knock off that fag stuff!'

'Better,' breathed Roper. 'Much better.' He gave a faint sigh and beamed at Vogel with a kind of amiable malice. His voice moved down into its darker, more sombre reaches. 'You must forgive my little jokes, Vogel. You think me very frivolous, I'm sure.'

'Not frivolous, Roper.'

'You disappoint me.'

'More . . . desperate, I'd say.' Vogel looked into the pale face and saw the thrust had gone home.

'But of course.' Roper gave a slow smile. 'What else?' He preened his hair. 'And now,' he said in a completely serious voice, 'let's get to that other factor.'

Vogel told him about the baffling orders that had come out of Washington that morning. When he had finished, Roper gave a low whistle of surprise. 'Just how important is Morrell?' he asked.

'Very. Don't ask me why he's so important, because I don't know. But in some way or another he's big.'

Roper frowned. 'And why the deadline, I wonder?'

'Your guess is as good as mine.'

'It's got to be tied up with their terms. But as we don't know their terms . . . The Ambassador hasn't been able to enlighten you?'

'Every day,' said Vogel, 'I give my Ambassador his little secret. Every day an Agency titbit, just to keep him sweet, even if I have to make the damned thing up. As a result, he's usually helpful, but this time it's no go. It may sound incredible, Roper, but I think the Ambassador's being kept in the dark, too.'

'Well, if the Ambassador doesn't know, and we don't know, who the hell *does* know?'

'Somebody knows, Roper. Somebody way up.'

'It's a problem,' said Roper. 'But I rather like problems.'

'Well, so do I.'

'Have to, don't we?' said Roper tartly. 'We get lumbered with them all the time.'

They grinned at each other across the table like two players at the end of a hard-fought set.

There was silence for a while. It was Roper who broke it. 'So what have we to go on? What's our edge?'

'Just the one thing: they don't know we're here.'

'That's a pretty big edge, Vogel.'

'Um.'

'But how the hell do we make use of it? You've got lots of men, I imagine, but it doesn't help, does it? We can hardly send in the Marines.'

'Hardly, Roper. Hardly.'

They had begun to sound like a couple of sinister comedians, polishing their act.

'Slip something into their drinking water? How about that?'

'I've thought of it. I don't like the idea.'

'The Company markets some very effective preparations.'

'Sure, but think of the risks. First, they aren't going to fall straight over. There's going to be an interval, however short, when they're feeling strange. Men can't be trusted at such moments, Roper. If they guessed the truth, they might well shoot the Professor. Even if they didn't guess, they might still shoot him. These preparations affect the judgement.'

'You think they'd really kill Morrell?'

'We have to reckon with it,' said Vogel. 'They've rubbed out a man of mine already.' Garen's sullen face came looming into his mind. 'Besides, what if they don't all take a drink of water at the same time? You'll admit that's a possibility, Roper? What then? Remember, sooner or later we have to go in there. We have to go in and pull the Professor out. Suppose there's one guy left on his feet. He's not been thirsty, or he drinks his scotch neat, or he hasn't touched anything but bottled mineral water since his mother told him about all those germs. That man is going to be waiting for us, and when we put in an appearance he's going to blow us to glory. Maybe the Professor, too. We can't risk a fire-fight.'

'OK, Vogel. Just a passing thought. Still, we do have to go in. Unless you decide against making any sort of move.'

'You jest, my friend,' said Vogel grimly. 'How would *you* like a posting to the Aleutians?'

Roper pulled down the corners of his mouth. 'That would follow?'

'As the night the day. Oh, it mightn't be the Aleutians. It might be Antarctica. How would you fancy that: chief of station on the South Polar icecap?'

'No, thanks. Penguins aren't my bag.'

'And could you blame them back at headquarters? It would look so feeble.'

'So,' said Roper, in a sprightly voice, 'we give it a go, Vogel.'

'It does appear that way, Roper.'

'I like it. Any idea how?'

'I suggest we keep things simple. It's always a good rule.'

'Sounds like a good old-fashioned break-in to me.'

'We could do worse.'

'But how?' said Roper, walking to the window. 'How? I see they've got the windows barred.'

'Yeah. They've done that.'

Roper looked at the ugly Edwardian house, the jumble of gables and chimneys, the foolish turret with its broken weather-vane. He began to whistle softly. 'Coal,' he said.

'What's that?'

'Coal. There has to be a cellar, Vogel. Look at those chimneys, a whole raft of them. There must be a big cellar. You know how it is with these old houses. And if there's a cellar, there has to be a coal-hole. A chute. Hang on.' Through the field-glasses, Roper examined the walls of the house at ground level. 'There it is! Behind those nettles.'

Vogel joined Roper at the window. He took the glasses. 'Just as I thought,' he said impatiently. 'It's barred, like everything else.'

Roper shook a finger at him. 'Too much central heating in your life, Vogel. A grille like that is meant to swing open. How else do you get the bloody coal in? Even if it's been fastened down, the fastening *has* to be on the outside. That shouldn't present much of a problem to a pair of competent technicians. What do you think? Simple enough?'

Vogel pulled a doubtful face. 'To the point of idiocy. But how much choice do we have?'

'We can get in there,' said Roper, his voice haughty. 'They aren't expecting us, don't forget.'

'*Me*,' said Vogel. 'Just me, Roper.'

The Englishman stared at him. 'I thought you might extend an invitation.'

'Going in there's a job for one man. And it has to be my job. I'm the one who'll be carrying the can.'

Roper pursed his lips. Then he gave a shrug. 'I suppose you could try flushing them out. How about a small conflagration?'

'Too risky. They might all fry. But smoke – that's a different matter. I'll take a couple of canisters along.'

'There's no justice,' said Roper. 'I get the ideas, and you get the action.'

'What's the big deal about going down a black, stinking hole into the possibility of lead?'

'For a desperate fellow,' Roper replied jauntily, 'it can have its charms.'

'I'll go down the burrow,' said Vogel, 'but you'll have your part to play. You can spread the nets. Take them as they come out. That has a charm all its own, don't you think? I'll give you the men for it. What do you say, Roper? Is that fair?'

'It'll have to do – but it lacks that touch of glamour which makes all the difference.'

Vogel stared at Roper. 'Crazy man!' he remarked.

They exchanged knowledgeable smiles. Despite their differences, Vogel and Roper recognized they had important things in common : both were hooked on danger, both understood the pleasures that can be found in the heart of fear, and both were natural hunters of men.

'Tonight, Vogel?' asked Roper in a light voice.

'Tonight, Roper,' Vogel replied.

They stood together staring at the house, a current of excitement passing between them. As they watched, a figure came out of the house and pushed open the doors of the garage. It was the dark young man. He moved cautiously, as if the light worried him. Roper's nostrils flared. He pointed a finger, the nail bitten to the quick.

Vogel loped over to the transmitter. 'What's the scene, Roper?' he called. 'Is he taking the car?'

'Yes,' said Roper, watching the young man intently. 'He's taking the car.'

Vogel gave the necessary instructions.

When David drove to London, he was being tailed. Vogel had put three men on the job. They had orders to observe him every minute, watch where he went, note any contacts he made, and make sure above all else that he did not gain any clue they were following him. They were three reliable men. No problems were expected.

'I wonder what business is taking that young fellow out,' said Vogel. 'And I wonder even more just when he'll get back. They're down to two, Roper.' He looked across at his new partner. Roper's face wore a veiled expression, as if his thoughts had gone far away. What's he thinking? wondered Vogel. He stared hard at Roper, much as he might have stared at some dangerous and exotic animal that had crossed his path in the bush.

19

David booked in at a cheap hotel near Regent's Park. He had chosen the place at random : he had never been there before and he would certainly not be coming back again. He was so occupied with his thoughts that the hotel made little impression on him. He was dimly aware of flowers in the hall, gleams of brass and copper, the smell of furniture polish, the fat face of the clerk smiling at him across the desk as he signed his name : 'Derek Shotover'.

He was taken up to his room in an old lift with wrought-iron bars. The room itself was absolutely anonymous : a faded blue carpet, a narrow bed, a wash-basin in the corner. On the wall there hung a seascape, which showed only waves, with never a ship in sight. David moved around the room like a ghost. To begin with, he rather welcomed the sensation of being adrift in a strange world, it made him feel as if he were invisible, but before long he started to become upset by it. He lay on the bed, troubled by the growing threat to his sense of reality. He stood up to resist the feeling and went walking up and down the room. He gripped the edge of the dressing-table till his knuckles showed white. He even tried to pray, but the words came echoing back to him out of empty space. Nobody was listening to the prayers of David Schuster just then – perhaps because at that moment David Schuster could hardly believe in his own existence.

He left his room and took to the streets, but that did not help, either. He could see plenty of people now, but he felt cut off from them, set apart by knowledge they could not share. He might have been an alien, walking the streets of a strange planet. He made his way to a news-stand and bought the latest editions of the afternoon papers. They told him nothing. Only Rachel and Moishe would have understood. He thought of them with longing, shut away in the ramshackle house, waiting for news. He had a strange mental picture of them. Rachel and Moishe were hunched in a small, brilliant cave of light, whilst the rest of the world spread round them, huge, dark, uncomprehending. How long would he have to stay away? Two days? Three? That had not seemed hard when they talked about it; now the time stretched to the horizon, vast and empty as a desert.

David was indignant at his sadness. He had expected fear and made provision in his heart against it, but he had not foreseen the loneliness which came upon him now, strong as grief. He wandered the streets, letting his legs carry him where they pleased, and woke from his daze with a start of alarm. Fantastic! Madness! He had been heading like a sleep-walker for Grosvenor Square – as if he meant to push open the glass doors of the American Embassy and deliver himself with his message.

'Crazy fool! What do you think you're doing?' He veered away east up Wigmore Street and wandered among the maze of buildings that runs off Marylebone Lane. These were unknown places to David. He passed shop-fronts, cafés, met impenetrable faces. The pavements reeled away ahead. At one point, he noticed the entry to a synagogue, its sober doorway only three steps from the road. There was a board fastened to spiked railings, and at the foot of the board, printed in gold letters, the words 'Dr E. Meyer, Rabbi'. David felt an urge to go inside the synagogue and pray, but after his earlier failure he did not think it would be within his powers. Besides, now wasn't the time for prayer. He had to make the call. David headed for the Underground station at Oxford Circus.

Two rows of phone-booths stood against the wall, identical boxes made of glass and laminated wood, all of them occupied just then. David loitered in the niche between the last of the boxes and the wall. The lights in the ceiling cast a pale unfriendly light on him. David felt very exposed, standing there. He watched the fret and bustle of the station, the escalators going up and down, the stairways full of people. It was all ordinary, yet all different.

An old woman in a flowered hat came out of the second booth from the end. Her face was crumpled and she was dabbing her eyes with a handkerchief. David hurried to take her place. He heard the door sigh to behind him and felt slightly more secure. He stood still for a moment, trying to calm himself, pretending to read the printed instructions above the phone. He knew the number by heart, he knew what he had to say, he knew he must be sure not to linger there after making the call, but he was finding it hard to keep these things properly arranged in his head. He took a deep breath and picked up the receiver.

A woman's voice replied. She told him she was the American Embassy and asked if she could help.

'The Ambassador,' croaked David. 'Urgent.'

The voice became defensive. It wanted to know his business. It explained that the Ambassador was a busy man. It suggested that a message might be left with his assistant.

'No,' said David, 'I must speak to the Ambassador. Now!'

The voice at the other end was puzzled. 'Look, could I have your name? Could you state your name and business?'

'Morrell,' murmured David. It sounded like a groan. His throat had almost closed up.

'Are you all right?' said the voice. 'If you're in some sort of trouble . . .'

'Morrell!' David bellowed the name down the mouthpiece. 'Professor Arthur Morrell.'

He was rewarded by an attentive silence.

'I'm speaking,' he said more evenly, 'on behalf of Professor Morrell.'

'I see. Could you hold the line?'

'Be quick!'

They were very quick.

'Hallo?' It was a man's voice now. 'Ambassador Brock here. Hallo? Hallo?'

David swallowed hard. His mouth was dry again, and for a moment he could not speak.

'Hallo! Hallo! Are you still there?'

'Yes,' croaked David.

'You have some news concerning Professor Morrell?'

Once more, like the time when he had walked into the College, David was suddenly set free from anxiety. It was as if he had to cross some boundary line and after that he left his fear behind. 'That's right,' he said. 'We're still holding Morrell. This is a reminder. You have less than four days left now. Do you hear me, Ambassador Brock?'

'Yeah.' A frozen monosyllable.

'Tell your Government if they want to see Morrell again they must follow our instructions. And quickly . . .' David's voice faded, his attention caught by what was going on outside the booth. There were people running across the hall. Somewhere in the distance he could hear the braying of a loud-hailer.

'Are you still there?' the Ambassador asked. 'Don't hang up yet. We need to talk.' The Ambassador's voice went plunging on but David found it hard to listen any more. 'How can we ascertain . . . ?' the Ambassador was saying. 'What guarantees can you give . . . ? How do we even know that Morrell's still alive . . . ?'

He's stalling me, thought David. The commotion outside was growing worse all the time. 'Morrell's all right,' declared David. 'He's alive and in good health. At the moment.' He saw with a thrill of terror that a policeman was coming towards the booth, moving fast, like a man with a definite purpose in view. 'Better act fast!' David yelled, and jammed the receiver down, just as the policeman swung the door open.

'Come out,' said the policeman. He looked nervous. There was a sheen of sweat on his forehead. His cap was not quite straight.

David stood still, paralysed with uncertainty.

'You have to come out.' The policeman grabbed hold of David's arm.

I've failed, thought David, with anguish. I've let us all down. I've stayed here too long and they've got on to me. He could see more uniformed figures running about the hall. The crowds had thinned away almost to nothing. Were they getting the place clear in case he started shooting? David became very conscious of the ·38 under his jacket. He stood there, his thoughts in turmoil, wondering whether he should go for the gun and make a fight of it.

The policeman's voice cut through his thoughts. It was a harassed voice. It was not threatening him, it was pleading with him. David forced himself to attend.

'There's a bomb,' the policeman was saying. His voice quavered as he spoke. He was frightened and he was trying not to show it. 'Our orders are to clear the station, sir.'

'The station?' echoed David, grappling with the man's words.

'Make your way to the exit as fast as you can. There was very little warning given.' He started to drag at David's sleeve again.

'Oh!' cried David. 'I see. Right!' He ran across the hall, his footsteps loud in the new silence, and as he ran, he caught sight of two men advancing slowly on a suitcase that was propped against the wall. One of the men was carrying some sort of metal rod in his hand.

David raced up the steps, giddy with fear, but wild with exhilaration at his escape. There were more police outside, herding people away from the entrance. David pushed his way through the crowd and went as far as the corner of Ramillies Street, where he paused to catch his breath. Just then there came a huge thudding bang. David felt the tremors strike through the soles of his feet. A cloud of dust rolled slowly out of the entrance to the Underground and hung in the air. People jostled along the pavement. A woman's voice jabbered nearby: 'Nothing left! That's what they say! Blown to bits! To rags!'

David felt his sadness returning. He wandered away into Soho. There was so little weight in his body that he seemed to be gliding over the pavement. 'A drink,' he told himself. 'That's what you need.' He went into a pub in Berwick Street and stood up by the bar. The barman served him a double scotch and then moved away. David looked round. The place was almost empty. Another impulse seized him. He would have liked to get drunk, very drunk. What was the saying in the Talmud about Purim? 'A man may drink today till he cannot tell the difference between "Blessed be Mordecai" and "Cursed be Haman".' David would have liked to do just that, but it was not possible. He had to keep his wits about him. Drink would loosen his tongue, cloud his brain. He wished there was somebody else to talk to. If someone came in, he decided, say a man on his own, he would try to strike up a conversation with him. Would that be sensible? Why not? Why not? What possible danger could there be in that? David felt starved for a word, a smile, a moment's recognition.

When the door opened, David glanced round hopefully. A young man came into the bar. He looked a decent type, clean shaven, blinking behind horn-rimmed spectacles. David gave him a half-smile. The young man did not seem to notice the smile. He peered round the bar and the tables, shook his head and left. David was disappointed. Soon afterwards he left, too.

The bomb had nearly thrown Vogel's men. In the confusion they lost contact with their target. It was just bad luck, a chance in a million, but they knew he couldn't have got far. They did some fast checking and their luck evened out. The guy was relocated, drinking in a pub in Berwick Street. It would take an earthquake for them to lose him now.

20

In the late afternoon of the same day, Moishe said he would try to catch a couple of hours' sleep. Before he went into the bedroom, Moishe asked Morrell to put his hands behind his back. 'No offence to anybody,' said Moishe, 'but I think this is the best thing all round.' He tied Morrell's wrists together.

Rachel watched the Professor's hands being bound.

'Sorry you won't be able to beat the young lady at chess,' said Moishe, 'but I'm sure you'll be able to pass the time somehow. You're a thinking man, Morrell, why don't you give your mind a little exercise working out the number of people that might be wiped out as a result of your experiments?' Moishe stared at Rachel. He was anxious to remind her that this man was not a harmless victim. 'All right?' he asked her.

'Yes.' She clutched the ·22 in her hand.

'I'll take the night stint,' promised Moishe as he went.

Rachel was left to guard Morrell. It was the first time she had done the job alone. She saw that the way Morrell's wrists were tied forced him to sit hunched forward. It made him hang his head as if he were ashamed. They sat together in silence. Rachel wished the whole business was over. Her thoughts kept turning towards David. She wondered continually what he was doing *then*, at that precise moment. He must have made the first phone call by now, she told herself. If only they would agree, implement the terms, this thing could come to an end and no more harm need be done to anybody. There had been no news so far. They had listened to the news bulletins but nothing had come through. The bulletins were taken up with descriptions of a bomb outrage at Oxford Circus Underground. One man had been killed, another injured. Rachel had been very afraid until she heard that they were members of a bomb-disposal unit. How many people in London? she mocked herself. Eight million? Those were the odds. All the same, she had been very scared that the dead man might be David. It took her a little while to find any pity for the man who had actually been killed. Then she began to wonder how people could do such a dreadful thing. What state of mind must the men be in who had planted the bomb? It was impossible to understand them. Then Rachel looked across at Morrell's bent head and felt a pain start around her heart. 'Please let it be over soon,' she prayed. Moishe had said that he did not expect any response yet, but she was worried by the lack of one. Besides, she was missing David a lot.

They sat like this for a long time and then Morrell started to groan. Rachel glanced across at him in alarm. 'Sorry,' she heard herself whisper. 'I'm sorry it has to be like this, Professor.'

Morrell raised his head at her voice and Rachel saw that his blue eyes were filled with tears. She watched the tears spill down his cheeks and the sight threw her into panic. It seemed so wrong. The only other man she had ever seen cry was David, but David's tears were shed in an excess of feeling : they were passionate, ecstatic, brilliant tears. Morrell wept dully, holding his face still, like a grieving statue. 'Please,' she said, 'don't.' Morrell was too big, too solid for tears. His features were too strong, too dignified. He was too old. The hair at his temples was grey. Rachel was deeply troubled by Morrell's show of weakness. 'Don't,' she urged him again, guilt appearing in her voice.

Morrell slumped forward on to his knees. Rachel stared at him, not knowing how to intervene, what to say or do. He shuffled over to her on his knees and laid his head in her lap. God! she thought, tormented. Like a dog! Like a pitiful old dog! Morrell was still crying. She could feel the heat of his breath through the material of her dress; the dampness of his tears spread on her skin like a stain.

Rachel looked down in anguish at the head with its bald

spot, the greying hair, the hands tied behind his back, their fingers working aimlessly. Morrell's head rested on her thigh. It seemed as heavy as a stone. Rachel felt deeply divided. Part of her wanted to push Morrell away, call for Moishe to restore the situation, but there was another part of her which was moved by the abandonment of Morrell's grief, and that was the part which won. Slowly, hesitantly, Rachel lifted her free hand to caress the grey hair. Morrell gave a sigh. He leant himself against her and he was so heavy that she had to straddle her legs to bear the weight of him. No, not like a dog, thought Rachel. He's not like a dog, he's like a child. A big, lost, frightened child. She could not help herself. She ran her fingers through Morrell's hair over and over again, almost as if it were David she were comforting.

Morrell was dreadfully tired. He had not slept properly since he was taken prisoner and his nerves were in rags. Now, with Rachel's fingers in his hair and her yielding thigh as a pillow for his cheek, he could almost have let go, almost have lapsed into sleep. There was nothing false about his tears. His misery was real, his longing for comfort overwhelming. His heart was filled with gratitude to Rachel for the kindness she was showing, but, even so, his brain did not stop its calculations. It was wondering whether he could take advantage of Rachel. Might she be persuaded to untie his hands? He did not dare frame the question. He could not find the words. He imagined her pushing him angrily away, thinking she had been deceived, abused. He could not bear the idea. It would not even reflect the truth. He was grateful to Rachel. Besides, his brain told him, he would lose all he had gained so far. Better to be still and surrender to those gentle fingers, knowing a bond was being forged between himself and Rachel that she would not find it easy to break.

'That'll be enough of that, I think!' Moishe's voice broke in upon Morrell. He had to endure Moishe hoisting him upright and pushing him into his seat. Moishe handled him brusquely but without open violence. 'Next time,' he said, 'I think I'll have to tie you to the chair as well!' He turned on

Rachel and gave her a questioning stare.

Rachel felt her face burn. 'I can explain,' she began, though she could not explain, not in any terms that Moishe was likely to understand.

Moishe waved her words away. 'It's all right,' he said impatiently. 'We all get screwed up sometimes. Why don't you go and have a rest?'

Rachel was glad to escape from the situation. She stretched out on the mattress in the bedroom and stared at the ceiling. She was not tired, her nerves were strung up far too tight for sleep. She was haunted by the memory of Morrell's tears, his head laid trustingly in her lap. She considered for a moment the awful possibility that the authorities in Washington might not agree to their demands, and then her mind went numb, it simply refused to work. A void opened in her head, and only by calling on David's name like a talisman could she defend herself, not against the blankness itself but against the obscene bloody thought she sensed still lurking in the midst of it. 'David,' she whispered. 'David.'

Rachel did not stay in the bedroom very long. She felt the need for company.

21

Vogel and Roper were getting ready to go into action. They had donned black sweaters and trousers and were wearing black plimsolls on their feet. Now they sat side by side in front of the mirror, daubing black grease paint on their faces and hands, looking like a couple of devilish clowns putting on their make-up before the show.

Roper could feel the excitement in his body. It was what he lived for now, this keen clear high. He could not do without it for long. He peered at Vogel's narrow face reflected in the mirror and gave an abrupt guffaw. 'Just look at you, Vogel! Some cultural attaché you turned out to be!'

Vogel worked the grease into the line of his jaw. 'The Apaches,' he remarked in a level voice, 'put on black paint when they wanted to advertise a killing of particular importance.'

'What sort of an answer's that supposed to be?' Roper gave his own reflection an encouraging smile. 'Where d'you come from, anyway, Vogel?'

'Texas, but it's been a long time. And you?'

'California.'

'That has to be bullshit, Roper.'

'It's true. Cross my heart. The California Estate. Outside Manchester.'

'Estate, eh?' Vogel pulled a woolly black hat down over his forehead. 'Sounds a pretty grand address to me, Roper.'

'Oh, it was. Very grand.' Roper let him thoughts dwell for a moment on the house. A house like all the others, one of the endless rows of red-brick houses, the place where his childhood had been spent. The California Gardens council estate. It had been built on fields that once belonged to the old parish work-house, a fact which had given the young Roper an unusual and instructive view from his bedroom window. He looked out on to black walls and towers and on to the cobbled courtyard below them. The casual ward of the workhouse had still been in operation during Roper's boyhood. He could remember the drunks and derelicts being herded out into the courtyard to split wood as a payment for their straw palliasse and plate of porridge. Those shuffling figures had haunted him ever since, hawking and spitting, blowing on their hands, peering up at him from ruined faces. 'Not me!' Roper had sworn. 'Never!' Just as he had sworn 'Not me!' when he thought about the lives of the people on the estate, the workmen in their faded overalls, the clerks and shop-assistants in their shiny suits, all coming out of their front gates at the same time every morn-ing. Even now the memory was enough to madden Roper. He felt he must have been *born* plotting his escape from that sort of existence.

Roper had no desire to linger over his early days. He banished them by springing to his feet, spreading his arms wide, rolling his eyes till the whites showed like those of a nervous horse, and going into a soft-shoe shuffle. 'Mammee,' he crooned, 'Mammee.' He began to laugh. 'Look at us, Vogel. We've been turned into nigger minstrels. The work of some particularly wicked fairy.' He danced some more, followed by Vogel's sardonic gaze. He felt a little drunk with expectation and only wished he were going into the house with Vogel. 'Dere might be locked doors,' he said, wagging a warning finger, still acting out his part as nigger minstrel. 'Can you-all cope, Massa Bones? Dat's what dis darkie wants to know.'

Vogel gave a measured smile. 'I can kingfish my way through any lock in creation. So long as I've got the kit.' He held up a worn leather pouch that chinked faintly. 'And I've got the kit.'

'Just make sure you drives dem varmints out. You hear me theah, Bones?' Roper dropped the act. 'Don't let me wait in vain.'

Vogel was buckling on a webbing belt, two of whose pouches held metal canisters. 'Sure, sure. Where d'you want 'em, Roper? Just say the word and I'll oblige. How about I send them out through the french windows for you?'

'Talk is cheap.'

'So be it!' said Vogel with a flourish. 'Through the french windows. Watch for them. They may even come.'

'Promises, Vogel. Promises.'

'We'll see.' Vogel was suddenly curt, as if he felt he had unbent too far. 'Time we were going, Roper.'

'Just as you say. At once – General.'

They had men posted in the shrubberies, covering all sides of the house, among them Pearson, the young officer who had found Vogel and Roper hand-wrestling. Pearson was in a cheerful mood, having been put in charge of the special sniper's rifle. It was a beautiful gun, a quiet weapon that would pick off a target cleanly with no danger of the bullet going through, a ·222 high-velocity rifle, fitted with night-sights so good they fascinated Pearson. Vogel had impressed on him that he must not bring his weapon into play unless things went bad and the situation became desperate. Pearson did not think he would get to do any shooting with the gun, but if he were called on, he certainly had the right equipment. He felt honoured to have been entrusted with it. The image-intensifier was excellent. Looking through it now, he was able to watch Vogel and Roper as they moved towards the house, even though the night was black dark, with the moon not yet up and the sky full of cloud. He saw the two figures go creeping forward, their feet groping among tree-stumps and tussocks of coarse grass. They gave him the impression of a couple of cautious arthropods fumbling their way along the sea-bottom. The image-intensifier showed a world with the colours of the ocean deeps, the light a sullen emerald glow, streaked here and there with bars of silver.

Pearson saw Vogel and Roper come to a halt and peer down towards their feet. For a moment, he could not understand what was causing the delay, then he made out the small slinking shape, black as the two men, except that when its head turned his way, he saw two eyes burning like green fires. A cat. It was rubbing itself against Vogel's ankle. He watched Vogel push the cat slowly away with his foot. The cat must have thought Vogel was playing some sort of game; at any rate, it persisted. Vogel dug his toe less slowly into its flank and after an uncertain glance, the cat turned its attention to Roper, winding sinuously around his legs. Roper scooped the cat up and threw it a couple of yards through the air. It landed expertly on all fours and stood peering at them. When the men moved forward again, the cat followed.

Pearson saw Vogel and Roper reach the house without incident. There had been neither sound nor movement from inside, nothing to suggest they had been noticed, only the usual light at the first-floor window, dim behind heavy drapes. Vogel and Roper squatted on their hunkers by the wall of the house.

The cat sidled towards them.

Some damn thing always had to come up, thought Vogel. He eased his body through the coal-hole and lay hunched across the shelving concrete funnel of the chute. When you went into action, always some crazy unpredictable thing. That, he told himself sourly, is Vogel's First Law. They might have expected some trouble with the grille but in fact it had presented no problem. Instead, they had been set on by a cat, the most persistently affectionate brute that had ever come Vogel's way, a shameless trollop of a cat, rubbing itself against their legs, singing like a kettle, presenting a ludicrous threat to the operation. Well, that followed. It followed. At the heart of things, Vogel reminded himself, there was a cosmic buffoon, a practical joker always ready to louse up the affairs of men. Vogel's First Law! In the end, Roper had been forced to pick the cat up and carry it away in his arms.

Vogel dismissed the cat and its implications from his mind. He let go of the grating and went sliding down the chute to land on the cold stone flags of the cellar floor, where he knelt on all fours, aware of grit under his hands, sniffing the air. He had come down into a different darkness. The atmosphere was stale and musty, the air lay like a stagnant pool. Vogel reckoned that nobody had been down here for a long time. It was a welcome thought.

He sent the narrow beam of his torch poking round the cellar. It picked out stone slabs, rough masonry, naked joists – and in the far corner, the beginning of a flight of steps that mounted steeply, turning out of sight. Vogel padded across the flagstones and began to climb the stone steps. At the head of the steps there was a door, put together from stout oak battens. Vogel stood still, listening, taking shallow sips of the unwholesome air. There was no sound from within the house. He tried the latch but the door would not move. Vogel nodded, took the pouch out of his pocket and set to work. The lock was a simple, old-fashioned mortice variety – no trouble to him at all.

The door creaked slightly as Vogel swung it open. Darkness lay beyond. Vogel listened again for sounds but there was nothing. His torch showed him he was about to enter a kitchen. He crossed the threshold and looked around him, taking particular note of the fact that there were two other doors opening off the kitchen, besides the one he had just come through. Vogel went to the nearer door and opened it a little way. Squinting through the crack, he found he was looking down a passage at the other end of which was the front hall of the house. A staircase mounted from the hall to the upper storeys. There was a dim light shining down the well of the stairs, not much, yet enough to make movement easy in that direction.

Vogel was satisfied by what he had seen, but he needed to know where the second door led. When he opened it, he found himself in a long, dark room. The torch picked out a couple of bulky, tattered armchairs and beyond them, in the bay at the far end of the room, a heavy mahogany table with a set of old-fashioned dining-chairs round it, two of them pushed out of place. The surface of the table shone under the beam of his torch as he approached. No dust, so the table must have been put to use recently. Beyond the table, the far wall was hung with heavy curtains. Vogel knew the curtains must hide the french windows but he twitched them open a little way to make sure. Right. OK. He remembered his promise and heard Roper's voice: 'Talk is cheap.'

There was another door in the room, piercing the inner wall about half-way down its length. Vogel figured that this door must lead out into the passage. It would give the room direct access from the main part of the house. Without it, the diners would have had to go through the kitchen or the french windows to get to table. Vogel tried this door. It was locked.

He stood in the middle of the room, stroking his chin, thinking about the situation. Then he returned to the kitchen and went from there out into the passage. He was following his own rule, which was always to adopt the simplest course of action that offered, the one which gave least chance to the practical joker who presided over events. Vogel's Second Law. He came to the foot of the stairs and stopped. From now on, there was no cover, not a vestige of cover, and there was no carpet to muffle his footsteps on the stairs. Was it a risk worth taking? With luck, he might reach the landing undetected, and then, if his luck still held, he might be able to walk in on the terrorists, take them by surprise and wrap up the entire business at a single stroke. On the other hand, if he were caught half-way up the stairs, he would have no chance at all. 'Try it,' he told himself, easing the ·38 out of its holster and setting his foot upon the lowest step.

Just as he did so, a furious spitting and yowling started outside. It made Vogel screw up his face in an agonized grimace. What the hell, he thought, was going on out there in the garden? Was Roper standing on the cat's tail? The outraged yowling came again, followed this time by the low rumble of voices overhead. Vogel got off the stairs fast and cowered against the wall of the passage. There was more talk, the sound of a door opening, feet clattering on the stairs. For Christ's sake, thought Vogel. They're coming down here! He gave a silent snarl and hunted round for somewhere to hide. His luck was in. He saw with immense relief that there was a cupboard opening under the stairs. Another moment and he was inside the cupboard, his feet groping for space among the heaps of junk. There was a broom handle poking into his back, a filthy duster lying against his left cheek, a sour smell in his nostrils. Vogel hunched awkwardly in the cupboard, his gun poised. He had stayed cool enough to leave the door open a crack so that he could see what went on outside.

'And this,' he told himself with desperate humour, 'is what they laughingly refer to as "playing it by ear"!'

Moishe was feeling restless and depressed. The mood had

come upon him gradually in the course of the evening, and though he had been reluctant to admit the fact, he knew the reason for it well enough. It had to do with Rachel and Morrell. It was because he had walked in and found them like that : Morrell on his knees before her, and Rachel consoling him, stroking his hair. The sight had set off a deep disturbance in Moishe's being. He tried to explain it in terms of Morrell's behaviour, his grovelling, his weak tears, his lack of pride, but there was more to it than that. Moishe knew he would never have been able to bring himself to beg for pity as Morrell had done, but that did not seem to him a matter for congratulation. He felt he might have put himself beyond the reach of pity for ever. He found he grudged Morrell the touch of Rachel's hand, he deeply resented it. Who was Morrell to be given such comfort? By what right did he claim it?

Besides, thought Moishe, trying to harness his feelings to a more practical frame of mind, it was always dangerous when a man lost control. It could lead to unforeseeable crises. In a moment of panic and misery, Morrell might do something stupid which would bring down on his head the death he so abjectly feared. As for Rachel, her behaviour seemed even worse. Few things could be more dangerous to them now than to give way to undiscriminating compassion. Moishe found it hard to forgive Rachel that. It seemed to him that her response had questioned the justice of their operation. It threatened the cause. 'But what is the cause?' he asked himself in sudden anguish. 'What is the cause, if it is not that the people may be established together in peace and love?' Peace and love. The words were bitter to him. He felt a deep sense of loss. He thought : I am a bit like my great namesake. I am like him when he was dying on Nebo : I can see the land promised to my people but I shall never get into it myself.

Moishe wanted to be able to condemn Rachel and Morrell and set the episode aside, but though his head was obedient, his heart was wounded and in revolt. His head agreed that their behaviour was a threat, but his heart told him it was understandable. It had the saving grace of human weakness, human compassion. Whereas he . . . Moishe's honesty drove him to admit that he was envious. The sight of Rachel and Morrell together like that had made him feel – lonely, horribly lonely. He had nobody to whom he might turn for comfort. His way of life, the actions that had been demanded of him, had seemed to forbid tenderness. He felt his heart was starved ground. Nothing could any longer put down roots there and live.

Moishe was tormented by these thoughts, which came crowding in on him, threatening the last strongholds of his resolve. He did not show his feelings to the others but they sensed his grim mood and fell silent. Memories returned to taunt Moishe, old deeds of violence whose iron demands had plundered his soul. The yowling, when it came, seemed like a part of them.

The screeching noise brought Rachel half-way out of her chair. 'God, what was that?' she exclaimed.

The yowling came again.

They looked at one another, searching each other's faces.

Moishe got to his feet. He was glad of an excuse for action. 'I think, only a cat,' he said. 'It sounded like one.' As he spoke, he remembered the black cat sleeping in the sun on the day they stormed the schoolhouse. It had never moved. It remained dozing, right through to the end when they carried out the corpses, as if it had been put there to show the indifference of Nature to all human affairs. 'Or two cats, more likely,' he added. 'Courting.' Moishe gave a bleak smile and drew the gun from his waistband. 'But I think we'll take a look round, all the same.'

Moishe turned to Morrell. 'Come on, Professor. Here's another chance to stretch your legs.'

Moishe did not consider it possible any longer to leave Morrell alone with Rachel. She might have a revolver but his hands were free, and anyway, she had proved herself so . . . emotionally gullible. 'On your feet, Professor,' he said curtly.

Morrell did as he was ordered.

Not until they were on their way downstairs did Moishe dig his gun into Morrell's back. He saw Morrell stiffen with fear and felt a moment's satisfaction, the nature of which he did not allow himself to examine.

Vogel was watching from the cupboard. At one moment the two men passed within a couple of feet of him, so close he could almost have reached out and touched them, but there was no action he could take. It was the big blond guy, the one who had killed Garen, and he had a gun stuck right in Morrell's back. Try to jump him and he would fire on instinct. Vogel watched the blond man change the gun to his left hand. It was a Smith and Wesson, a ·38 Special, not a weapon to be taken lightly. The man took a key from his pocket and unlocked the door that led from the passage into the dining-room. He and Morrell went inside. Vogel noticed with interest that the gunman had left the key in the door. A moment later, the two of them came back out of the room again. It looked as if they were just making the rounds. Vogel watched the gunman lock the door again and then push Morrell ahead of him past the cupboard towards the kitchen. Vogel suffered a few moments of suspense, because although the cellar door was shut, it was no longer locked. Would the gunman notice? The footsteps coming back towards Vogel lacked urgency. The kitchen must have been given only a cursory glance.

Once more, the gunman and Morrell passed through Vogel's line of sight. Vogel peered at Morrell's face, trying to assess his state of mind. The Professor did not look as if he could be relied on to do much for himself, even if the chance of escape were offered. Morrell's features showed that sullen, dazed expression which Vogel recognized from past experience as the face of chronic fear. Well, he thought, you couldn't blame the man. He had been through a lot. Vogel listened to their footsteps going back up the stairs and waited only a little longer. His plans were made. He reckoned he might even be able to keep his promise to Roper about the french windows. He hoped so. Failing that, he would have to take advantage of the general confusion. Vogel came out of the cupboard and began his preparations.

He found that the door between the kitchen and dining-room was fitted with a bolt, so he did not even need to use his tools to jam the lock. He made a rough estimate, then fixed the timing device on the second of the canisters, setting it to go off five minutes after the first. The moment had come for doing what you must and hoping that the practical joker up there would not happen to be looking in your direction. 'Let's roll it,' whispered Vogel to himself, and felt that secret spasm, that pulse of pleasure which comes to initiates of violence when they begin what they know must be a crucial act.

'There's a smell,' said Rachel. 'Like something burning.'

Moishe sniffed the air. Certainly there was an acrid odour, faint but definite. He glanced round the room. Nothing seemed wrong, but even so the smell was growing stronger all the time. Moishe walked over to the door and pushed it open. Hazy veils of smoke confronted him, drifting up the well of the stairs and hanging in the open space of the landing. The sight awoke deep alarm in Moishe. He knew how disastrous a fire could be for them. If the place really caught alight, they could do nothing but make a run for it – a blaze would bring fire-men, police, reporters. If they had to run, everything they had achieved so far would be put at risk. There was no other safe house available; Morrell might easily make his escape in the confusion; they would lose contact with David; the whole operation could go down in ruin.

'Here!' cried Moishe. 'Both of you! Quick!'

Rachel and Morrell ran out to join him on the landing.

'What's happening?' asked Rachel. She saw the veils of smoke. 'Is it a fire, Moishe? How could a fire get started?'

'You're going to have to help me,' said Moishe to Morrell. 'Unless you fancy getting roasted.'

'Anything. I'll do anything I can.' Morrell sounded almost eager.

'Stick close to him, Rachel.' Moishe cast a fierce glance at

Morrell. 'And no nonsense, Professor. Now, come on, both of you.'

As they ran down the stairs, Moishe tried to answer Rachel's question. 'Started? I don't know. Maybe there's an electrical fault. Old wiring. I don't know.'

They reached the passage and saw thick whitish smoke seeping out from under the door that led to the dining-room. Moishe rammed the key in the lock, threw the door open and flicked on the light. Smoke stood in the room, as thick as a wall. Moishe went plunging into the livid glare, the other two following close behind him. 'We've *got* to find what's causing this,' shouted Moishe, and then began to cough as the smoke hit his lungs.

From his hiding-place in the cupboard, Vogel watched them go stampeding through the door and allowed himself a private smile of congratulation. As he had foreseen, the key was still in the lock. During the first few seconds, while Moishe and the others blundered round the room, Vogel emerged from the cupboard, crossed the passage, pulled the door closed and turned the key. Then he stood back and gave the door a nod of approval. It was a stoutly built article. To break down such a door would not be easy, even if a man didn't happen to be choking with fumes and half-blind into the bargain. The door to the kitchen was just as strong and he had shot the bolt firmly home. Oh, those fine old craftsmen of former days, thought Vogel, rocking with sardonic glee. They certainly built things to last!

By Vogel's reckoning the second canister should start to blow any second now. And that, he thought, almost tenderly, should be that. He went to the place he had already chosen for himself, a position just inside the kitchen, which allowed him to overlook both exits to the dining-room at once. Hearing the moans and cries and paroxysms of coughing that came from inside the room, Vogel felt deeply satisfied. He had them in the trap and there was only one way out. 'Take it!' he urged them silently. 'Take it!' He very much wanted to keep his word to Roper. Somebody began beating first at one door and then at the other. Vogel held his position, waiting. In his judgement, the only person with any chance of breaking the door down would be the big fair-haired guy, and Vogel reckoned he would be able to nail him comfortably as he came staggering out. Once that was done, the rest should be easy. But Vogel did not think any doors were going to be broken down that night. They were too strong. The people in the room had only one escape route left and that was through the french windows. According to plan.

'Are you ready, Roper?' murmured Vogel. 'I hope you're ready, my cat-trampling, degenerate English friend. Because it can't be long now.'

One of the armchairs in the room was pothering fiercely. Smoke was coming from it in what seemed to Moishe impossible quantities. There was an instant when Moishe stood in the white glare, bemused by the sight of the chair, another in which he remembered the yowling of the cat – and suddenly, he *knew*. He knew, and as if to confirm his knowledge the second armchair erupted. Smoke began to blow from it in a fierce white jet. Moishe stood among the fumes, dazed, as the survivor of an earthquake might stand among the ruins of his house. One minute they had been safe, the next they were plunged into disaster. He had no doubt about the trap. Some kind of malign web had been spun round them unawares. For a few seconds the knowledge took away Moishe's will to act.

By now Rachel was hauling furiously at the knob of the door. Morrell stood beside her, head down, hacking into cupped hands. Rachel began to beat on the door-panels with the butt of her gun. 'It won't open,' she cried to Moishe, her face contorted, her cheeks streaming with wet.

'Stop that!' said Moishe. He pushed her aside and threw his shoulder against the door. As he feared, it would not budge. He squinnied up his eyes and leaned his head against the jamb, trying to force himself to think. Meanwhile, Rachel had gone running over to the other door, the one that led to the kitchen. Moishe followed her. She found that this door would not open, either. Moishe could have predicted it would not.

Rachel began clawing at his shirt. 'Get us out of here,' she pleaded. 'I can't breathe, Moishe.'

'Listen to me,' said Moishe, covering his mouth and nostrils with one hand. 'You have to understand, Rachel: this is no accident.' She seemed unable to take his words in. 'Please,' she cried again. 'Get us out!' Then she was struck by an idea. 'The window!' she exclaimed, coughing. 'The french window. We could get out there.'

'No!' yelled Moishe. He got her by the shoulders and swung her round. If one avenue of escape had been left conveniently open, Moishe knew they must not take it. If they did, that would be the end of them. No, they must try to outsmart their opponents. Moishe struggled to think of a way. He looked at the others through watering eyes. Both of them were in bad shape and Moishe knew their condition could only grow worse. A few more minutes and they would all be completely disabled. He heard Morrell start to retch and dug his fingers into the flesh of Rachel's shoulders. 'Listen,' he said again, his voice thick, 'we can't go out that way. There'll be somebody waiting.'

'The french windows,' she cried again. 'What's wrong with the french windows? Let go of me, Moishe!'

He shook her savagely. There was very little time left. 'Don't you understand? They'll be waiting for us.'

Moishe felt Rachel stiffen. ' "They"?' she faltered, choking on the word. 'What do you mean, "they"?'

'I mean we have to find some other answer.'

Rachel seemed to understand. She looked at him with brimming, bloodshot eyes, and then she pointed. He followed the direction of her finger and thought, Of course! I am a fool! He peered at the picture, the crazy picture that hid the hatch. It was possible . . .

'Lie flat,' he urged Rachel, pushing her to her knees. 'And stay close to the Professor.' A quick glance showed him that

Morrell was already stretched out on the floor, wheezing and coughing into his hands.

Moishe went towards the hatch, his eyes swimming so much it seemed to him as if the room was melting. He was resigned now, his spirit had found bottom. He had come to terms with the catastrophic reversal of their fortunes, he had admitted the likelihood of their failure, and by accepting it he had been granted an ultimate calm. He had been here before, in this lucid empty quarter of being. He had watched the same sort of calm take over in other people, mortally wounded men as they sank towards the grave. Moishe was not sure yet whether he would die, but he had become reconciled to the possibility. The knowledge sharpened every nerve, turned away his fear. It was the last gift of life.

Moishe told himself that if he could find his way out of the room, at least the element of surprise would return to him, the scales would tilt that bit more his way. He was acting on the assumption that their assailants were waiting to grab them as they came out into the garden, but he could not ignore the fact that somebody might still be lurking in the house. After all, it was no disembodied spirit that had penned them in the room. Moishe gave a moment's thought to the resource of such an operator. Formidable! But how the hell had all this come about? How had they *known*? Moishe dismissed the question from his mind. Holding his gun in his right hand, he used the left to slide back the cover of the hatch a little way, and there, in the blurred aqueous twilight of the kitchen, his eyes made out a shadowy figure. Moishe fired at once, and saw the man twist away and go scuttering through the door that led down to the cellar. Moishe was not sure whether he had hit the man, but he thought not. He swung himself out through the hatch, dived for the cellar door and rammed the bolt home, all in one urgent movement. Once he had the intruder shut up, he spun round and began to advance warily up the passage. It was empty. Nobody challenged him. Moishe gave a harsh, wheezing sigh of relief. His wheezing reminded him of the others and he made haste to unlock the dining-room door. Rachel and Morrell came crawling towards him on all fours. They appeared to be in really bad shape but he could not spare the time to help them yet. He ran up the stairs and kicked open the doors of the other rooms. There was nothing in any of them. It looked as if only one man had come in, the one he had shut in the cellar. It made sense : a single infiltrator to set the trap and the rest of them waiting in the garden, ready to pounce when the smoke drove their victims outside. Moishe was weighed on for a moment by the idea of hostile presences out there in the dark. A fit of coughing shook him and he saw that smoke was still rolling up the stairs, so he ran back and shut the door of the dining-room. Rachel and Morrell were slumped on the floor, their backs propped against the wall. Both of them looked groggy. 'Keep an eye on the Professor,' he urged Rachel. 'We really need him now.'

Rachel stared at him, ashen-faced. She gave a nod, but he wondered just how much she understood. Had she grasped the terrible questions raised by this invasion of the house? Moishe's thoughts turned to the man who had run down into the cellar. Would he still be there? Most likely not, thought Moishe. Most likely he had come in that way and would make his escape by the same route. Still, thought Moishe, he ought to check. He felt ashamed of himself for being so careless. He could easily have tightened the security of the place but he had been so sure they were in the clear. So sure . . .

His thoughts were moving very fast now. The idea of going down those twisting stairs into the dark cellar did not much appeal to Moishe. He cast round for an alternative – and found one. Covering his face, he plunged back into the reek of the dining-room where one of the chairs was still blowing clouds of smoke. Moishe grabbed the stinking chair and dragged it across the passage towards the cellar. Once there, he leant over from the cover of the wall and slipped the bolt back. Before his next move, he sent a bullet through the battens, in case the man should be lurking on the other side. Then, in one galvanic burst, Moishe flung open the door and tipped the chair down the cellar steps. He had a glimpse of it trundling downwards, rocking and swaying, spewing white smoke, and then he banged the door shut and ran the bolt back home. That should speed the bastard on his way – that, or else choke him! Moishe would have very much liked to question the intruder, but he realized the man would probably be clear of the house by now. He went back to see how Rachel and Morrell were faring, and helped them up the stairs to the living-room. Morrell was still far from well. His breathing sounded like an asthmatic's at the height of an attack. 'Bad chest,' he wheezed, as Moishe propped him in a chair.

'Tough luck,' said Moishe, but all the same he tied Morrell's wrists and ankles. The man was their last safeguard now. Without him they would never get out of this business alive. Everything had suddenly become very much more tricky, yet as long as they held Morrell, thought Moishe, they could still win.

Because of Morrell's weak chest, Moishe went and opened the windows, but now he had to take care not to expose himself to any marksman who might be stationed in the garden. Oh yes, he thought, it had all become a lot more tricky now.

Rachel lay sprawled on the mattress and her face had the dazed look of somebody in shock. Moishe frowned and went down to the dining-room, where he made an examination of the armchair. Inside its stinking carcase he found what he expected. He dragged out the spent canister, wrapped it in old newspaper and hid it on top of a high cupboard in the kitchen, where Rachel would not be likely to find it. Moishe foresaw bad times ahead. No more delicate manœuvring. The game had changed. It would be bare-knuckle stuff from now on, stomp and gouge. Just then, the phone on the landing began to ring and Moishe realized he had been waiting for that to happen : it was standard procedure. He went to answer it.

'Yes ?'

The voice that spoke to him was light in colour, faintly epicene. An English voice. 'I think,' the voice said pleasantly, 'the time has come for us to have a little chat.'

142

Moishe grunted.

'How are things at your end? Professor Morrell's health remains good, I hope?'

'Morrell's OK. Apart from the smoke in his lungs. He suffers from a bad chest. Did you know that?'

'Oh God! Unfortunate. Could I possibly speak to Morrell?'

'Not now.'

'We need some reassurance, you understand.'

'Not now. Take my word, he's all right.'

'Super!' The voice was pliant, quick to defer. 'That's really super.'

Moishe frowned at the mouthpiece. 'Super'? What kind of talk was that? 'How about you, then?' he said, malice entering his voice. 'How is our caller's health?'

'Him?' There came a whinny of laughter. 'Oh, he's back with us, you know. No real harm done.'

'Pity.'

'By the way,' said the voice, 'I shouldn't advise you to leave. It might get a little rough if you try. We have lots of people about.'

'No intention of leaving,' growled Moishe. His throat hurt when he talked. 'You know,' he said, 'you people made a real botch of things tonight.'

'True.' The voice sounded penitent. 'But in these affairs so much depends on luck.'

There was a pause.

'Anything you'd like to ask?' the voice resumed. 'Any supplies you need? Don't hesitate to make your wants known to us. We've no wish to harass you, we're only concerned for the safety of Professor Morrell.'

'I bet!' Moishe replied grimly. For a moment, he was tempted to ask the question that had been haunting him ever since the attack was made, but he knew better than to raise the subject himself. After all, it was possible that they did not know about David. It was possible – though in that case, how in God's name had they found the house? Better to say nothing. If they had picked David up they would be sure to

143

try and use him in some deal. Moishe reckoned they would let him know. 'Have you anything to tell *me*?' he asked hoarsely.

'No,' said the voice. 'Not at present.'

Moishe put down the phone.

When he went back into the living-room, Rachel was on her feet, waiting to confront him. 'What was that?' she demanded.

'Nothing.'

'You were on the phone. I heard you. Was it David?'

'No, not David.'

Rachel looked anxiously at him. 'Moishe – is David all right, do you think?'

'David? Sure he's all right. Why not?' Moishe cleared his throat. 'Listen, Rachel,' he went on. 'We've still got Morrell, so nothing has changed.'

'Nothing? Tell me what happened down there. Who did that to us?'

'I don't know. Somebody got in. Could have been a tramp.'

'Don't take me for a total fool, Moishe. They've found us, haven't they?'

Moishe gave an uneasy shrug.

'But how? How could they know?' Rachel's voice faltered again. She peered at him with bloodshot eyes.

Moishe tried to reassure her with a smile. 'There could be a thousand reasons. Maybe we were seen, Rachel. Maybe we left clues around, things we know nothing about. It's easy enough to do – and these people are smart operators.'

'Not David?' she asked in a breathless voice.

'No.' Moishe shook his head vigorously. 'David's in the clear. I'd bet my last penny on it.'

'You're being honest with me?'

'Sure I'm being honest.' He saw how desperately she wanted to believe him. 'From now on, Rachel,' he told her gently, 'it's best if we take things as they come up. Not go looking for worries.'

She nodded but she still persisted. 'When they spoke to you on the phone – did they mention David at all?'

'No,' said Moishe. 'They definitely did not. I give you my word. Which makes me absolutely certain he's OK.'

'Thank God!' cried Rachel. 'Oh, thank God!'

Behind her fervent relief, Moishe could sense the doubts still lingering, but he did not think Rachel would dare bring them out into the open again. That would be like encouraging them.

'You got through, then?' said Vogel.

'We had a little preliminary talk. Quite satisfactory, as an opening gambit. Which is more than can be said for the rest of tonight's work.'

Vogel pulled a sour face. His left arm stung where the bullet had nicked it. He fingered the dressing thoughtfully. 'And Morrell? He's still OK?'

'Approximately. Did you realize, Vogel, that our Professor has a weak chest?'

'Weak chest?' Vogel cast his eyes towards the ceiling. 'Weak chest! Oh boy!' That was a very neat touch on the part of the universal practical joker. Vogel gave a sigh. He had just had to send a depressing dispatch in code to Washington reporting on the failure to free Morrell. Never mind, he thought glumly. Things could be worse. At least the Professor was still breathing, even if he wasn't doing it too well.

'You know what?' said Roper. 'You should have taken me along.'

'Oh, sure. You and the cat both!'

Roper accepted the rebuke. 'Total balls-up,' he said, falling into a dreamy, musing voice.

'They'll call it that now,' said Vogel sharply, 'but if things had gone well it would have been a very different story. The operation would have been hailed as a model of its kind, a triumph of resource and courage.'

'Um?' said Roper vaguely. 'What's all that about?'

'That, my friend,' said Vogel in his most cutting voice, 'is Vogel's Third Law.'

Roper looked at him for a moment and then began to laugh.

22

When the news arrived the President was in bed. He had already put in a fourteen-hour working day and he got up grudgingly, but he did get up. He knew this was business which would not wait. According to his instructions, the message had been brought to him direct. There were no intermediaries beyond Hagan, who had taken the report out of the hands of the ciphers office and done the de-coding himself. The matter could only be pressed to a successful conclusion if complete secrecy were maintained.

When Hagan had first spelt out the news he felt a shiver of pleasure go through him. Political necessity was lining up on the side of his personal predilections. He experienced a kind of hungry awe, realizing what must follow. Overweening pride, he told himself, was about to get its come-uppance.

'Well,' said the President, smoothing the grey spikes of his hair with a big hand. 'Our men didn't manage it, George. They didn't get Morrell out.'

'No, Mr President, it seems they didn't.'

'Which would appear to narrow our options down to one.'

Hagan waited, his breathing quick and shallow.

'He's a man of great abilities,' the President remarked in a tender, rumbling, bass voice. 'A pity he let it all go to his head. A terrible shame when a man like that abuses the privileges of office. It's all there in the file, George. Can't be denied. All the same, can I do this to him?'

Hagan understood what was required. 'Other considerations apart,' he said, trying to strike the same rueful note as the President, 'we have to take into account the long-term failure of his policies.'

'Failure, George. That's a hard word. A merciless word. Are

146

you sure you're being fair?'

Hagan became flustered and felt the need to make his points very quickly. 'The Secretary's gotten most unpopular in the country,' he asserted. 'You've seen the newspapers, Mr President. Seen what they call him: "The spendthrift of American prestige." "The prodigal son of American diplomacy." "The man who put the States in second place." '

'*Some* of the papers, George. Do you agree with those opinions? As a historian?'

'They have . . . some foundation, I'm bound to say.'

The President sighed. 'Then maybe what's happened has all been for the best.' He shook his gaunt head. 'Such abilities! It's a shame when a man of that stamp is corrupted by money – and that'd be the angle to stress, George, the financial-peculation side of things.'

Hagan nodded, bright-eyed behind his spectacles.

'So we ditch him.' The President was suddenly brisk. 'Now, George, this matter is as sensitive as a sore prick. You'll have to handle it with great . . . tact. Know what I mean?'

'I think so.' The imagery did not much appeal to Hagan, but he knew the President occasionally lapsed into such talk during moments of stress.

'About the leak,' the President went on. 'It has to be completely indirect, George. By which I mean there has to be no way in which the White House can be implicated. I'll tell you how I want this news to break.' The President leant back in his chair and smiled. His manner became almost playful. 'I want to get it hot and strong in tomorrow morning's papers. I want it splashed by some fearless newshawk in the *Times* or the *Post*, some investigative journalist, the kind of man who can't be gagged. You know, George, there's a lucky fellow out there who's about to make a big name. Well, we should all be grateful to the watchdogs of the Press, and that's a fact.' The President cleared his throat. 'Once the news breaks, I shall do what I have to do. It'll mean the Secretary's immediate suspension from office. He'll be out of the job by noon. That's a hell of a fast schedule but we have the deadline to consider.'

The President pushed the skin of his forehead into thick corrugations. 'I suppose you've heard it said, George, that politics is a dirty game?'

Hagan moistened his lips. His heart beat faster. 'There is a certain undeniable . . . expediency in politics,' he remarked in a judicious voice, his thoughts turning eagerly towards the kill.

'And then,' said the President, his manner suddenly fierce, 'we must make sure we can't be compromised from the other end.'

'Other end?'

'The minute we have the Professor safely in our hands . . .' The President paused. 'Those people – who are they, George? Those terrorists. What organization?'

'That's not become clear as yet.'

'Then it looks as if we'll never know. A pity, in a way.'

'Sir?'

'*They* won't be telling us.' The President stared heavily at his aide. 'Neither us nor anybody else, George.' He paused a moment to let his words sink in, and then continued, 'We must never leave anyone in a position where they can stand up and accuse the United States government of coming to secret accommodations, bowing to terrorist pressure, stuff of that sort. It would be the end of us politically. That's leaving aside the matter of retribution. They can't be let live, George. That's the long and short of it.'

'I understand,' said Hagan hoarsely.

'Good. Then you'll also understand what I'm going to say now. These terrorists have got to be removed from the scene fast. They must never get as far as a court-room, George, nor even an interrogation-chamber. There must be absolutely *no* hobnobbing with them. Why,' said the President, shaking his head at the idea, 'just think of the fantastic accusations they might level at the Administration. Charges so fantastic they might catch the public imagination.' The President gave an ambiguous smile. 'It'd be Goebbels's "big lie" all over again, eh, George? Far better such people be terminated, speedily and in secret.'

Hagan stared at the President. He was deeply impressed.

'I'd like you to send the necessary instructions right away, George. Leave the details to the Agency. They've handled this kind of request before. And burn the demand-note, too.' The President's mood seemed to change. 'Such a waste!' he said. 'Such a tragic end to a great career! It's going to be hard for me to let this happen, George. I shall hate doing it. Be sure you make the leak with the utmost discretion.'

'You can bet on it, sir.' Hagan heard the eager thrust of his voice and tried to counter it by looking sad. 'I'll go set things up without delay.'

'And I'll go back to my bed,' announced the President. 'Just one more thing,' he called, as Hagan went towards the door.

'Yes, sir?'

'We never had this conversation, George. It did not take place.'

Hagan swallowed hard. He blinked at the President from behind his spectacles. Then he nodded slowly and left the room, his steps on the parquet rather less buoyant than they had been when he arrived.

23

Vogel rejoined Roper, who was drinking coffee laced with whisky in the thin light of the dawn. Both men had cleaned themselves up: Vogel was now deployed behind a suit of British bespoke tailoring while Roper had gone back to his leathers and jeans.

'Want some?' asked Roper. The bruises under his eyes looked darker than ever, as if they had soaked up the black grease he had wiped off elsewhere.

'That'd be great.' Vogel slumped into a chair.

'What's the trouble?' said Roper with barbed innocence. 'You sound a bit down.' He handed Vogel a steaming mug. 'Paddy coffee, thick but strong.'

Vogel took a drink. 'That's better. Christ! I've got a mouth like the bottom of the parrot's cage.'

'Spare me the grisly details! How's the arm coming along?'

'It's on the mend, thank you. How's the cat, Roper? Managed to tread on it again?'

'I've tried, Vogel. I've tried. You know, that's a deeply mysterious cat. It keeps waiting for me in the shrubberies.'

'Probably got a yen for you.'

'Unlikely,' said Roper with a venomous smile. 'It's not even a tom.'

Vogel refused to let himself be provoked. He stared down at his coffee. 'New orders have come through.'

'Well?'

Vogel gave a sigh. 'They're really making things tough for us, Roper. I wish I understood their thinking. They've set us a big problem.'

'Another? We get nothing *but* problems. Well then –' Roper fixed his grey eyes hungrily on Roper's face – 'let's have it, General.'

Vogel pressed his lips together with vexation. 'I'm told the terrorists will be prepared to treat now. I'm told that, but not why. We're to make a deal with them, Roper. We get Morrell, and they get safe-conduct to a country of their choice.'

'So where's the problem?'

'The problem arises because we don't mean to . . . implement. As soon as we have Morrell, we close them out. Immediate.'

'Vogel, dear lad, they won't just . . .'

'Oh, I know. I know.'

'They're going to ask for another hostage before they let go of Morrell. Somebody to make the trip with them. They'll absolutely insist, Vogel.'

'Sure. But they can't have another hostage. And there's not going to be any trip.'

Roper gave Vogel a probing glance. 'I have got this right? You do mean what I think you mean?'

'Yep. The measles. Fast.'

' "The measles," ' echoed Roper in a caressing voice. 'You know, I'm a great admirer of the phraseology your people use.' He frowned. 'But why, Vogel?'

'Orders from the top. Like I told you, they didn't give me reasons.' Vogel rocked his body uneasily to and fro. 'No attempt at capture. Just . . .'

'Say it, Vogel. Do me a favour: give it me in the official wording.'

Vogel shrugged. ' "Termination with extreme prejudice." That make you happy?'

'Delighted.'

The two men stared hard at each other.

'Your people,' murmured Roper, 'are so good at thinking up those elegant euphemisms. I wonder what poet minted that one.'

'We're a nation of immigrants,' said Vogel. 'I guess we lack your easy command of the *mot juste*.'

'How true! But I see what you mean: we certainly do have a problem. There's one word you've mastered!'

'Shall we get down to it, Roper? Without any more shenanigans?'

'At your service,' said Roper in his more sombre voice.

'Well, what have we got this time?' Vogel became brisk. 'What we've got is three terrorists. Two of the terrorists are shut up with the Professor, and they know all about us by this time.'

'They have good reason to.'

Vogel ignored this remark. 'We've achieved communication, in that instance. Did you talk to them again, by the way?'

Roper nodded. 'I persuaded them to put the Professor on the line for a moment. He sounded a little like a concertina but otherwise he appears to be all right.'

'OK. Good. And the phone to the house is tapped. Now,' said Vogel, 'we come to the third terrorist. This young man is roaming around London, doing bits of business, making threatening phone calls to the Embassy. Obviously their link-man. We have him under observation but he doesn't know it. He hasn't been in touch with the house since last night's events, so naturally he still thinks they're in the clear . . .' Vogel's voice faded. A long silence ensued.

'I think we've come to the end of the easy bit,' said Roper eventually. 'The fact is, these people aren't going to let go of Morrell unless we give them somebody else.'

'We can't do that.'

'I don't see how the hell we can avoid doing it.'

'Listen,' said Vogel. 'Any man sent in there might as well pack his death-certificate. That big blond guy is a rough customer. If he went, he'd make sure he took the hostage with him.'

'Any men you feel you could do without?' asked Roper in a glinting voice.

Vogel looked at him coldly. He was remembering Garen, dead by the side of the road. 'I've lost one officer already,' he said. 'One is enough.'

'Ask me nicely, General, and I might go in for you.'

'Stop the fooling, Roper. There's a problem here and we have to solve it. Another bad egg and I'd be really inconvenienced.'

' "Inconvenienced," ' said Roper, savouring the word, rolling his eyes up towards the ceiling. 'You'd be inconvenienced all the way to the Aleutians.' He looked keenly at Vogel but there was no response from the American.

Vogel and Roper sat at the table, their chins in their hands. They were silent for about twenty minutes and then Vogel began to shift restlessly in his chair like a man who is being visited by interesting thoughts.

Roper looked at him, eyebrows raised.

'Maybe . . .' said Vogel to himself. 'When you weigh one thing against another . . . Nothing is foolproof, but we might be able to swing it. I think we have to try.' He drew in his breath excitedly. 'Roper,' he said, 'I just had myself an idea.'

24

David found it hard to sleep that night. The ashtray by his bed filled up with cigarette butts, his throat grew dry, and when he finally managed to doze off he was harassed by a dream. He woke from the dream to a strange window and a view of damp mauve roofs.

In the dream, David had been at home in his father's house. He was looking out of the bedroom window on to a garden that was different, much bigger and wilder than Mr Schuster's real garden. There was an old rose hedge screening the far end of it, and beyond the hedge stood dark woods. As David watched, a gang of dwarfish figures came scuttling out from behind the rose hedge and started off down the path towards the house. Somehow, David knew they had come out of the woods, from burrows in the hillsides. The dwarfs did not try to hide themselves and yet their movements were furtive. David noticed one of them had a rifle slung over his shoulder. As the dwarf with the rifle got nearer, he seemed to realize that David was looking at him. At any rate, he turned his head towards the window and gave a knowing grin. He had a wickedly elated face, the jaw thrust out, the eyes glittering. David saw that the whiskers on his cheeks were dense and short, like the fur on a beast's muzzle.

In the dream, David gave a cry of dismay and immediately Rachel was beside him. She took one look through the window and clapped her hand to her mouth. 'Oh,' she exclaimed in disgust. 'Like rats!'

The dwarfs went scuttling away behind the garden shed and there the dream ended – or rather, David forced himself out of it at that moment.

He got up, draped the shawl round his shoulders, put on the skull-cap, and began to pray, but once more David's prayers seemed to lose themselves in a void. He wondered with a stab of panic whether his faith had deserted him. Had God removed himself? Was the Holy One denying them his support because of what they had done? Surely not, when everything had been intended to help preserve the land and the people? Then why, thought David, could he not pray? He felt badly in need of advice and there came into his mind the name of Dr Meyer, the name he had seen yesterday on the notice-board outside the synagogue. Would it help to speak to a teacher in the faith? As soon as he asked himself this question, David knew he would go talk to Meyer. He searched for the rabbi's telephone number in the directory and found it. Perhaps the rabbi sensed the tension in David's voice. At any rate, he agreed to see him without delay.

David felt much more cheerful once he had arranged this meeting. He went straight out on to the streets without bothering about breakfast. There were a couple of other things he had to do before he saw the rabbi. First, he bought a range of morning papers and worked through them. There was no evidence in them so far that the American government might be going to accede to their demands. David was worried, even though he remained convinced of Morrell's enormous importance. Surely, he thought, they wouldn't abandon him to his fate? These thoughts led David to put in another call to the Embassy. He repeated his warnings and was answered by a voice whose controlled venom chilled his blood. David was not used to hatred yet. He knew it was crazy, but he could not help feeling hurt by the hostility the voice showed towards him. He made his way quickly towards the rabbi's house.

Dr Meyer proved to be a man of stocky build who carried himself in an assured, considered way. He wore the features of his race, if not with pride then certainly with confidence. He gave the impression of being a man who was both physically and spiritually prosperous. His black beard accentuated the fullness of his lips; his nose was hooked. There was no appeasement in his face, no circumspection; it was the kind of face that had been handed down with little change from those desert tribesmen who had been present, millennia ago, at the foundation of the House of Abraham, a wilderness face, stamped even now with the memory of fierce suns long ago.

Dr Meyer welcomed David and led him into his study, a much-lived-in room whose walls were lined with books. David stared in awe at some of the volumes. They were old and venerable, bound in such stout leather that it looked as if their makers had foreseen an eternity of consultation. David was reminded by the books that the kind of man his race had most revered over so many centuries had not been the soldier nor the man of business but the scholar, deeply versed in the Law. It was the men of learning who had held the people together and preserved their identity in the far-flung settlements of the Diaspora, they who had brought about the miracle of Jewish survival. It had needed the deepest resolution to act as they had done, the most absolute trust. It had meant flying in the face of reason, but, thought David, if men like Dr Meyer had not persevered over so many years, he would not have been able to stand there at that moment in the rabbi's study and pronounce himself a Jew.

Dr Meyer asked him to sit down. 'Tell me,' he said, 'what it is you wished us to discuss. You have a question, a *sheila*, perhaps?'

David found himself at a loss where to begin. 'I've only lately come back to the faith,' he said. 'My parents are not observant. Not at all. They brought me up – well – like a heathen, a *goy*. That's what they wanted for themselves.' He stopped, shocked by the depth of bitterness he heard in his voice.

'Better not to condemn,' said Dr Meyer. 'They are your parents. They brought you up. They cared for you. What you tell me is nothing new,' he added. 'In every generation, some fall away, but enough go on.' He gave a smile. 'We generally manage to keep a *minyan*. Better to be glad that you have found your way back. Who knows? They may follow.'

David shook his head. He could not lay claim to any such optimism. 'I am very ignorant, Rabbi,' he said. 'In need of advice. Often I become confused. Things get mixed up in my head. Sometimes I waver in my faith.'

'And who does not? These days it is common.'

'Tell me, Rabbi,' said David, trembling. 'Are we Jews truly the elect of God?' The question sounded terribly abrupt.

'We have that obligation,' said Dr Meyer, choosing his words carefully. 'Can you doubt it? Reflect upon our history.'

'I have done. Sometimes it seems to me like no more than catastrophe piled upon catastrophe.'

'Surely not? Well, yes, perhaps. That is the history of all nations, taken in the long run. We Jews look farther back than anyone else. We have been witness to the fall of a number of eternal empires. I think it would be more accurate to regard our story as one of miraculous survival. And remember, we still go on.'

'Where do we stand now, Rabbi?'

'I have no doubt,' said Dr Meyer, 'that it remains our destiny to establish the ideal law of God in the world. It always was our destiny. It has not changed.'

'And Israel?' said David breathlessly. 'What is Israel's role?'

'Israel?'

'The state of Israel.'

Dr Meyer smiled into space as if some benign vision had manifested itself there. 'The return to Zion,' he said, 'is the most profound aspiration of the Jewish race. For that to be accomplished, Israel is vital.'

'And what if Israel were lost?'

'Lost?' Dr Meyer gave him a wounded glance. 'How should it be lost?'

'You must agree, Rabbi, it has many enemies. It could go under.'

Dr Meyer stared at him, pain showing in his eyes. Then

he said in a resolutely humble voice: 'I cannot believe that will ever happen.'

'But suppose the danger arose. What steps would a man be justified in taking to preserve Israel?'

'Where are you trying to lead me?' asked Dr Meyer. 'You understand a rabbi must accept responsibility before God for those who follow his judgements?'

'You won't answer me?'

Dr Meyer shrugged. 'I will try to answer you.'

'Are there any limits to what a man might do?'

'Of course there are limits. A man,' pronounced Dr Meyer, 'could take all steps within the Law.'

'Violence? He could use violence?'

'Force of arms. Yes. But you know all that. When Israel was established, we left behind the era of the Jewish victim.' Dr Meyer's voice rose. 'The gathering-in has begun. It will continue. Meanwhile, we have to defend the Land by all lawful means.'

'Israel,' said David, 'is not Zion. Israel is a secular state.'

'Israel is a secular state but we are a divinely appointed nation. Out of Israel the true Zion will flower.'

'You believe that?'

'How else should I go on?'

'But if Israel were cut off before its flowering?'

'Unthinkable,' said Dr Meyer. He began to rock back and forth as if in prayer. 'That it should be delayed again! Unthinkable!' He closed his heavy-lidded eyes.

'Thank you,' said David. 'You have helped me very much. I was feeling very confused. Very much alone.'

'There is,' said Dr Meyer with weary dignity, 'a *historic* loneliness in being a Jew. You should bear that in mind.'

'I understand, Rabbi. You have been very kind. I won't take up any more of your time now.'

'I am still not sure about this,' said Dr Meyer as he saw David to the door. 'I am not at all sure that you have asked me the entire question that was in your mind, and so I cannot feel confident that I have answered it.'

'Enough of it,' said David. 'I asked enough and you told me enough. I'm happy with the answer.'

Dr Meyer frowned. 'Here,' he said, picking up a booklet from the hall-table. 'Take this with you, David. It is a recent commentary for laymen on the *Schulchan Aruch*. Which,' he added, 'also began its life as a commentary for laymen. As you may know. Well,' he said with a smile, 'that is our way. The Jewish way. Caro? *The Ready Table?*' He put the booklet into David's hands. 'It will help you when you are troubled.'

They stood together on the doorstep and Dr Meyer began to make another observation about the booklet, but suddenly David stopped listening. Another voice had caught his attention, that of a news-vendor on the corner. The man was shouting magical words:

'American Crisis. Secretary of State falls.'

David could not bear to stand still a moment longer. He broke away from the rabbi and began to run towards the corner. Dr Meyer watched him go sprinting away, shook his head and went back into the house. He was wondering whether the young man might not perhaps be a little unbalanced in his mind.

David could not find any change so he took a pound from his notecase, thrust it at the newspaper-seller, and snatched up a copy of the paper. There it was, strung across the page in banner headlines! A line of massive black print:

SECRETARY OF STATE RESIGNS:
GRAVE CHARGES

David blundered away, not caring where he was going, his eyes running feverishly across the lines of type: 'Dramatic disclosures . . . evidence of corruption . . . President's expression of grief and shock . . . End of an era . . .' Great God, they had done it! They had done it, blessed be the Name! David felt his spirits go soaring upwards. They had toppled him. They had cut off the head of Holofernes. They had brought Haman down. Such an occasion, said the Talmud, should be a time for feasting, the exchange of gifts, the succour of the humble. Oh yes, yes! David walked the streets of London in a daze of joy.

He bought several different newspapers, as if each new copy somehow established a little more certainly the truth of their success. Eventually, he found himself wandering in Green Park and did not have the slightest idea how he had got there. He sat down on a bench to study the reports in more detail. The need to concentrate calmed him down a little, but every now and then a spasm of excitement would go shooting through him, strong enough to make his fist clench and crumple the paper in his hands.

He savoured the words of the political commentators: 'This should not be seen merely as a personal débâcle,' he read, 'but as the end of those policies of *rapprochement* which have come under increasingly hostile scrutiny in recent months . . . Some of the secret clauses commonly thought to have been included in the Secretary's treaties have had the effect, no matter what their intention, of endangering America's traditional allies and upsetting the military balance . . .' How true, thought David. What excellent fellows these political commentators were! What good sense they wrote! How enlightened they were, all of a sudden!

David sat on the bench in Green Park, weak with happiness. It took him a while to bring his feelings under control. He told himself he had to be practical. There were still the final arrangements to make. He must go and buy the airline tickets and then he would phone Moishe and let him know that everything was ready. He could imagine the jubilation they must be feeling, back there at the house. He saw Rachel in his mind's eye, her face shining, transfigured. Later, he would take the Rover back to the house and pick up Rachel and Moishe. Morrell would already have been put under heavy sedation, according to plan. By the time the Professor woke up, the three of them would be in Amsterdam, where Moishe had friends who could be depended upon, if need be. And then – it would all be over! There would be nothing more to fear, no more threats, no more killings. Moishe had told them he would be staying in Amsterdam for a while, but David and Rachel would fly as soon as possible to Israel. It was a great victory the three of them had won, David knew that, and although they could never speak openly of the matter to others, every breath he and Rachel drew in Israel would be made precious by the secret knowledge that they had helped preserve the land from destruction. 'Halleluyah!' he cried, jumping to his feet. A woman walking a Pekinese dog stared at him suspiciously. David got himself back under control and went hurrying away. He left the tract on the *Schulchan Aruch* lying forgotten on the bench, under the pile of newspapers.

25

Moishe heard the news on the radio and a fire seemed to scorch his body. His lips drew back in an exultant grin. He called Rachel through into the bedroom, his voice choked with emotion, and they stood together listening to the voices of the newsmen, with Rachel clinging to his arm. The commentators stropped their beaks, feeding on calamity. They were rarely thrown so rich a carcase as this.

'We have *busted* him,' exclaimed Moishe. He smashed his fist into the palm of his hand. I am still good for something, he thought. He had helped turn the tables on one of the men of power, one of those people who had brought such depriva- tion to his soul. Moishe's spirit settled into a triumph that went beyond joy or grief. He felt he was in some high place, raised above the turmoil of the world, left to enjoy a great silence.

He drove the feeling grimly away. Their victory was not final yet.

Rachel was talking to him. 'David will know by now,' she was saying anxiously. 'He'll have heard, won't he, Moishe?'

'Yes, he'll know by now.' Moishe gave her a smile of unusual sweetness. 'There's no need for you to worry.' He had assured Rachel so often that David was all right, he had almost come to believe it himself. Now, suddenly, it began to seem more likely. 'I shall have to arrange things with them,' said Moishe, pointing through the window. 'I'll see we all get away together.' At that moment, he felt that there was nothing he could not do.

He walked back into the living-room and gave Morrell a big grin. 'Well, Professor,' he said, 'you are a great man after all. A very important fellow.'

Morrell ignored these remarks. 'Could you help me?' he said, his voice heavy with humiliation. 'I must get to the toilet. I want to go there really badly.' He was still trussed hand and foot. The ropes around his legs had to be untied before he could make his way to the lavatory.

'Sure,' said Moishe, in great good humour. 'A pleasure to be of assistance to such an important man.'

'Be quick, Moishe, would you?' urged Morrell.

'So you're taken short. Well, that's all right. We'll get you there.' Moishe bent down and began to undo the knots around Morrell's ankles.

The phone rang. When he heard it, Moishe stopped what he was doing.

'Please. Be quick,' said Morrell.

Moishe saw Rachel run out on to the landing. He hesitated, then decided to let her go. He knew who would be calling. They had phoned him a couple of times already that day. He understood their motives. 'Tell them I'll talk to them in a minute,' he shouted. As he spoke he heard Rachel give a cry of pleasure. 'David!' she exclaimed. 'David, it's you!'

Moishe abandoned Morrell and ran out on to the landing.

'Yes, yes, it's wonderful — ' Rachel was saying. 'Absolutely incredible . . .'

Moishe snatched the phone out of her hands. 'Listen to me,' he said urgently. 'This is Moishe. Don't come back here, David. You hear me? *Don't come back to the house.* I'll be . . .'

There was a click and the line went dead.

Moishe glanced at Rachel. 'All right, then,' he said into the emptiness. 'I'll tell her that. Better ring off now. See you, David.'

Moishe put down the receiver and smiled at Rachel. 'He sends you his love,' he lied. 'You do understand,' he continued, 'that it would be unwise for David to come here at the moment. I have to arrange things first.' He hid from her the fact that the call had been interrupted.

Rachel looked at him with mild reproach. 'I would have told him myself.'

'Don't worry. I'll see to everything. When we come to terms, I'll make sure that David joins us.'

Rachel looked up at Moishe, smiling, thankful, ready to give him her entire trust. No harm had come to David. Moishe had been right all along.

They went back to the living-room and found that Professor Morrell had not been able to wait the extra few minutes. He had soiled himself in the meantime and now sat abjectly in his own rising stink.

Moishe tried to offer him some comfort. 'Never mind, Professor,' he said. 'It's not your fault. My apologies for inflicting such a thing on you.' He finished untying Morrell's legs. 'Let's get you cleaned up.'

Just before he led Morrell to the bathroom, Moishe said to Rachel, 'If the others should call – ' he nodded towards the window beyond which, somewhere, their besiegers lay hidden – 'I want you to fetch me at once. We can make a deal with them now. And I think we should make one, fast.'

'Oh yes,' said Rachel. 'Let's do that, Moishe. Let's get it over with.'

'Rachel,' said Moishe. He spread his arms and gave her a brilliant smile. 'Rachel, we *won*!'

David was bewildered and upset by Moishe's words. Don't come back? Why not? It did not make sense. When he was talking to Rachel she hadn't said anything like that, then

Moishe had come suddenly barging his way on to the line. Not a word about their success. Only that single baffling order – after which he'd rung off without another word. Very strange. David wondered whether he could possibly have misunderstood what Moishe was saying. Then a new question raised itself in David's mind. Moishe, he thought, is a tense, desperate sort of man. Could he have cracked up? Might *he* have been the one to break under the strain? If that were the case, would Rachel be all right with him now? Could she be in any danger? David's joy shrivelled. He was seized by doubts.

He tried phoning the house again but the line seemed to have gone dead. What the hell was happening? David knew that he would have to go and see in person. He would be careful. He would park the Rover a couple of streets away and make the rest of the trip on foot, but he would have to go, despite what Moishe had said. He could not stay away from Rachel any longer. God, how sickening, he thought, to have this kind of worry just at the moment of success.

David took a taxi back to the hotel and settled his account there. Then he drove away in the Rover, heading north-west. Every move he made was reported on, just as all his other moves had been reported during his brief stay in Central London. When he got to the house, David would be expected.

'How soon do you think they'll ring again?' asked Rachel. She was wandering restlessly about the room.

'Don't get too near the window,' said Moishe.

Rachel paid no attention. She seemed drawn towards the window. Her eyes strayed over the area of rough grass to the sprays of Michaelmas daisies that had survived in an overgrown border. She looked at the empty drive, the long shadows thrown by the afternoon sun, the gable of the house across the way, rising above grimy shrubberies. 'It looks so quiet,' she said. 'Is there really anybody out there? I can hardly believe it.'

Moishe grunted. 'You'd better,' he said. He was playing

chess with Morrell again. It was a way of shielding himself from Rachel's questions. Whilst Moishe played, his brain was busy working out the terms he would ask and the way in which the exchange could best take place. He would need another hostage as a substitute for Morrell, but he did not think they would jib at that, nor at anything else he asked, not now, when they had just admitted the huge importance Morrell had for them.

Moishe gave a sigh. This kind of dying fall to an operation was always troublesome. It was hard to stay alert. There was a temptation to let go. The game was already won, you felt, so it was easy to lose your sharpness; but neglect of detail could still be fatal, at least so far as they were concerned. Nothing could put back the great Humpty Dumpty they had knocked off his wall. The Secretary of State was finished. A phrase of Scripture drifted into Moishe's mind: 'Canst thou draw out Leviathan with a hook?' Well, they had done it. They had hooked Leviathan!

David remained a source of worry, one Moishe dared not disclose to Rachel, but on reflection he did not think the problem of David was so crucial. Even if they had picked David up, he could still be made part of the exchange. Danger only arose if they hid the fact that they had seized him. It was quite possible David was still free, in which case he would be sure to call again. The men outside would have to be persuaded not to tamper with the phone next time. Moishe very much hoped that David was still at large. He did not know how far he could rely on Rachel to keep her nerve if David became part of the bargaining. He wished the opposition would be quick and phone again so that he could establish the position about David with them. Things were a little tricky but they were certainly not out of control. Moishe's thoughts moved on to the type of plane they would need and the precautions they would have to take in the business of the exchange.

'It looks so ordinary out there,' said Rachel. 'You feel you could just walk down the drive and back into the world.'

'I wouldn't recommend it,' said Moishe, then shook his head reprovingly at Morrell. 'The knight,' he said. 'You were meant to take the knight, Professor.'

'Ah. I never noticed,' said Morrell. Moishe had freed his hands for the game but his ankles were still bound.

'Try not to lose so obviously, Professor. I mean,' Moishe went on with a wry grin, 'try to do it with more consideration for me as a player.'

Morrell smiled back. He could sense that the tension had diminished among his captors and felt that the threat to his own life had grown that much less. He did not understand why this was so, and he thought it wise not to enquire, but he was becoming more and more convinced that he would survive. He knew that Moishe was in contact with their besiegers and guessed it could only be a matter of time before some sort of bargain was struck. His chief fear now was that the men outside might try another rash move.

'I'll do my best for you,' he told Moishe. Now, as his confidence grew, he found himself enjoying the wry humour of the big blond man and responding to it genuinely. Also, he remained grateful to Moishe for the way he had helped him through that humiliating episode when he dirtied his pants. He was wearing a pair of Moishe's trousers at that moment. In fact, Morrell found himself thinking quite fondly about both the man and the girl. He had lived very close to them for a while now and there was no denying that it did create a bond. He had come to know them as people, human beings rather than ferocious stereotypes, people with different temperaments, different fears and weaknesses. They had taken on names for him now. He thought of them as 'Rachel' and 'Moishe'. He had even taken to calling them by their names sometimes, just as they would address him as 'Professor' or even 'Prof'.

'I'll do my best to oblige, Moishe,' he said again. He saw that by taking the knight he would expose his rook.

'The exchange favours me,' said Moishe, removing the rook from the board. 'That surprised you, eh?' Moishe shook his head. 'Ah, Professor, when shall I find another opponent like you? I'm going to miss our chess games. Tell you what,' he added, with the air of a man making a generous concession, 'the next one we'll play straight.'

'Ohhhh,' came Rachel's voice, a dreadful strangled wail. Moishe jumped to his feet, turning over the chess board as he went. He was beside Rachel in a moment. Her face was chalk white, stricken. She was pointing through the window. Following the direction of her finger, Moishe saw a slim figure hesitating at the end of the drive. It was David. Moishe cursed under his breath. David walked slowly forward, trying to look casual, as if nothing more than idle curiosity were leading him up the drive.

Suddenly, Rachel threw the window open. 'David!' she screamed. 'Run! Run for it!'

Moishe clapped a hand roughly over her mouth. 'Shut up!' he barked. It was possible they might have let David through, but after Rachel's cry, the danger to him had become very great. David had heard Rachel's panic-stricken voice and it had awoken his own fear. He glanced round the silent garden, jerking his head this way and that, like a frightened bird. Moishe waited, frozen with suspense. It might be all right. It could still be all right. He saw David rear away, his right hand going into his jacket. 'Keep clear of the gun!' urged Moishe silently. He became aware of Rachel. She was moaning again, her mouth wet against the palm of his hand.

David's attention seemed to be fixed on the shrubberies. They must have called on him to halt, thought Moishe. David did not halt. He backed off fast, and as he did so, he drew his revolver. Moishe heard his own voice yelling 'No!' and saw flame leap from the muzzle of David's gun. Once, twice; the reports were like wood snapping. 'Oh no!' cried Moishe again, seeing David stagger. They must have returned fire.

David tried to run, but after he had taken only a couple of lurching steps, a strange glazed weariness stole over him. He stood as if perplexed by what had happened. There was no more firing. The silence seemed to open on David like a huge mouth. There was neither sound nor movement from the shrubberies. In the distance a car hooted. Somewhere nearby a bird was singing. David started to sway. He took a step to regain his balance, but once the movement was begun he could not control it and went reeling across the drive, back in the direction of the shrubberies. 'Rachel,' he cried in a thin plaintive voice that slurred and wound down at the end, like the voice of a tired child, begging for help. Then his legs buckled and he fell face down among the potholes of the drive, only a yard or two from the dark shrubberies.

Watching this, Rachel and Moishe both became absolutely still. They saw David's shoulders twitch once, and then he lay motionless, stretched out among the lengthening shadows of the garden.

The noise began deep in Rachel's throat. Moishe held on to her tight, his hand still clamped against her mouth. The noise was sorrow, raw and bleeding sorrow, without dignity, without even a human presence, a noise rising out of the well of the past, older than mankind, a howling that made Moishe's scalp crawl and the hair bristle in the nape of his neck.

'Please, Rachel,' he begged her. 'Please,' but there were no words that would serve.

The howling went on.

David's body lay where it had fallen, looking like a heap of old clothes.

Moishe tried to turn Rachel's face away from the window and she bit him savagely in the side of the hand. Moishe gave a grunt of pain and let her go. Blood welled up through the teeth-marks. For a moment, Moishe was able to think of nothing but the pain and in that time Rachel ran to her handbag and got the ·22. 'I'll kill him for that,' she wailed. 'I'll kill them all.' She was beside herself, the eyes rolling madly in her head. 'Where is he?' she cried, blundering round the room. 'Where's he gone?'

Moishe saw that Professor Morrell was no longer in his chair. He had taken refuge under the table and was squatting there, his chin on his chest, his fingers locked across his head, hunched like a foetus, absolutely still. Drunk with desperation as she was, Rachel could not find him. 'God, God!' she moaned, lurching against the sideboard. 'This can't be real.' She began to howl like an animal again, waving her gun dangerously round the room.

Moishe launched himself on her and caught her in his arms. For a moment she fought him, but then she went limp and dropped her head on Moishe's chest. Moishe worked the gun out of her fingers. Even now, at this moment of shock and anguish, he did not let himself forget that Morrell must stay unharmed. Moishe wrapped his arms round Rachel, holding her close to him, rocking his body slowly to and fro, trying in this way to offer her some consolation. After a while, she grew quiet. She lifted up a tear-stained face to him and whispered, 'Moishe. Tell me it isn't true.'

All he could do was look away.

'Oh, Moishe.' She raised one hand to her head and began to drag at her hair.

'No,' he said. 'Please, Rachel.' He untangled her fingers and stroked her hair smooth. The blood oozed from the heel of his hand on to her scalp. He watched the blood dully, holding her to him, trying to give her comfort.

The telephone began to ring.

Moishe let it ring for a while but he knew it must be answered. 'Professor,' he called hoarsely. 'Professor.'

Morrell slowly lifted his head and craned out from under the table.

'There are some tablets in the drawer of the sideboard, Professor. Would you get them for me, please?'

Morrell looked down miserably. He gestured to his bound ankles.

Moishe sat Rachel down in a chair. Still holding her with one arm, he reached into his pocket and took out a clasp-knife. 'Here you are,' he said. 'Free yourself, Professor.'

Morrell took the knife, opened it, and sawed through his bonds. He got to his feet, blinking, fearful, a weapon in his hands.

'The tablets,' said Moishe. 'And some water.'

Morrell hesitated a second and then did as he had been asked, placing the bottle of tablets and the glass of water down carefully upon the table before folding the knife and handing it back to Moishe, an action he performed slowly and resignedly, like a man surrendering his sword.

The phone was still ringing.

'Rachel,' said Moishe gently, 'I want you to take a couple of these.' He showed her the bottle of tablets. They had been meant to drug Morrell at the end of the operation. 'Will you take them for me?'

Rachel looked at him with huge blank eyes.

'Please, Rachel. It's for your own good.'

Finally she gave a nod.

Moishe fed the tablets into her mouth and she did not try to spit them out. After her raging grief she seemed to have fallen into a stupor. Her limbs hung slack. She had turned into a weary, obedient child.

'Drink,' said Moishe. 'There's a good girl.'

Rachel did as he asked.

The phone rang on and on.

'I'd better answer,' said Moishe. He knew delay might lead the people at the other end to wrong conclusions. 'I'll be back in a just a minute,' he assured Rachel. She lay in the chair like an exhausted child. 'Look after her, Professor. See she does herself no harm.' Moishe gave Morrell a searching glance. 'I rely on you,' he said, and went out on to the landing.

The phone stopped ringing. Morrell could hear the murmur of Moishe's voice. He sat down beside Rachel to keep her company. Her eyes were closed but tears seeped slowly from under the lids. Suddenly she opened her eyes wide and turned them on Morrell, and he winced at the glittering, spiked, bejewelled anger that flashed in them.

'I wanted to kill you,' she said in a flat voice.

'I know. I understand. Rachel, I'm awfully sorry for what happened.'

'Sorry!' She could hardly mouth the word. 'He says he's sorry!'

'What else can I say?' pleaded Morrell.

'They killed him. Your friends killed him. Say that!'

Morrell was silent. He could hear the mutter of Moishe's voice and hoped he would come back quick.

'You'll be going to America now,' said Rachel in a dreamy tone. 'You'll be safe – and David will be dead. That's what's going to happen, isn't it?'

'I don't know.'

'Yes. That's what'll happen. You'll go back to the woman you love.' Rachel gave a shuddering laugh. 'What's her name, Professor?'

'You mean my wife?'

'Not your wife. That girl. Your mistress.'

Morrell shook his head guardedly. He would not answer her question. How did they know about such matters, he wondered. A terrible suspicion began to make headway in his heart.

'I'll tell you her name, shall I?' said Rachel. 'It's Judith.' She flung the word at him like a poison dart. 'Do you love her very much, Professor?' Rachel went on. She had begun to sob. 'You do love her, don't you? Love her and trust her? Because – she's the one!' Rachel thrust a tormented face at him. Like a wounded animal, she was lashing out against the monstrous pain. 'Judith Glass passed us the information. All about your research, Professor. Your secrets. Judith Glass. That's why we knew to take you. What do you say to that?'

Morrell stared stonily ahead. A treacherous landscape stretched before his eyes, sown like a minefield with betrayal upon betrayal. His life, the picture of his whole life! He had not escaped it. Nothing had changed. Judith had never loved him, either. A groan came from his lips.

Rachel stared at him and, even in her anguish, she felt suddenly ashamed to have dealt him such a blow. 'I would have shot you if I could,' she said as if to explain. 'I wanted to . . .' Remorse and desperation mingled in her voice.

'So you did this instead.' Morrell nodded. 'It'll do. It's near enough.'

'Hallo,' said Moishe.

There was a different voice at the other end of the line this time, an American voice, using a slow, relaxed drawl which all the same could not quite purge itself of anxiety. 'Let me tell you this,' said the voice. 'Let me assure you of this fact. What happened just now was a complete accident. It was never our intention. But he used his gun and my officer felt obliged to defend himself.'

'That's your story.'

'It's the truth. We are very sorry it happened.'

'But he's still dead,' Moishe said bitterly.

'May I remind you,' said the voice in a tone of exquisite diffidence, 'that this is not the first man to have been killed in the course of the present action.'

'True.' Moishe was grim. 'So you reckon that evens up the score?'

'I didn't say that.' The voice paused. 'In my opinion, we ought to settle matters before there are any more accidents. I think we should trade. What do you say? You are,' the voice enquired delicately, 'willing to trade?'

'Yes. We're ready.'

'In a *position* to trade?'

'We haven't hurt Morrell, if that's what you mean. We aren't savages in here.'

'Then I suggest we negotiate.' Relief showed clearly in the voice. 'We could start talking things over right away.'

'An hour,' said Moishe. 'Give me an hour.'

'The sooner we start . . .'

'An hour. I need an hour.'

'But why delay?'

'Don't "but" me,' growled Moishe,

'All right. An hour then.'

'One more thing . . .'

'Yes?'

'Move the body. Get it out of sight of the house.'

'That's already been taken care of,' said the voice. It was soberly respectful, the voice of an undertaker. 'We wanted to avoid causing anyone needless distress.'

'Damn you!' said Moishe, provoked by the voice. 'I know what you think you're doing.'

'How do you mean?' asked the voice quickly.

'Don't try to soft-soap me. Don't give me any more of your oily talk. That doesn't work with me. All it does is make me mad.'

'Sure,' said the voice soothingly. 'Sure. An hour, then.'

Moishe banged down the receiver.

He went back to Rachel and tried to encourage her as best he could. Soon, he knew, the sedative would take effect. Meanwhile he held her hand tenderly in his and sweated to prove to her that they must go on. They must, he argued, take the operation through to a successful end. They owed that to David. It would not be worthy of David's memory if they failed now. David had died in support of a great cause and his sacrifice should not be diminished in any way. The two of them must stay alive so that they could fight again. David would have wished it to be like that.

He pursued these arguments for quite a while and saw Rachel was beginning to listen to him with stony-eyed calm. The drug was working. In the end, Moishe felt able to say: 'Rachel, I love you as a comrade, a sister, and I grieve with you as a member of the family. I will stand by you. And remember, David was a man who had faith. Remember, the dead are never dead to God. There is Paradise.' Moishe did not believe his words about God and the hereafter. They were his father's beliefs. He borrowed Jacob Hartmann's faith and made an offering of it to Rachel. He was able to do so now because love had sprung like a freshet in his parched heart at the sight of Rachel's grief.

'There'll be no proper mourning for him,' said Rachel slowly.

'Listen,' Moishe urged her. 'We will say *kaddish* for David in Jerusalem.'

Rachel lifted his hand to her lips and kissed it. 'I don't care whether I live or die,' she told him in a drowned voice.

'Then you must live, Rachel. It's our duty to live. We, above all people in the world!' Again Moishe remembered his father as he spoke. These were the old man's convictions he was voicing.

Rachel nodded. She even gave a wan smile. Moishe saw that she had mastered her grief. Her face was composed. Resolution showed in her voice. 'I'll do as you say, Moishe,' she told him. 'You can rely on me from now on.'

Moishe flung out his arms and embraced her.

26

'All right,' said Vogel down the phone. 'We can do that for you. Certainly.' He found his effusiveness disgusting. He sounded like the manager of some two-bit store, falling over himself to satisfy the whims of a customer. 'Of course, you realize this is going to take a little while to arrange.'

'Make it by late afternoon tomorrow,' said the guttural voice.

'Do our best.'

'Make it!'

'All right. Now I'd better just run through the items again. Just as a check. First, you want a light plane.'

'Piper Comanche. Full tanks.'

'Of course. Full tanks. We wouldn't try to . . .'

'Get on with it.'

'A pilot,' said Vogel, his voice silky as he restrained his anger. 'The pilot will fly the plane. He will also act as hostage in exchange for Professor Morrell.'

'Agreed.'

'The plane is to lie well out on the field. It will have to be a small private airfield, you understand. A place we can take over for the duration of the operation.'

'Right.'

'You want a sandbagged bunker to be put up near the plane, the walls of the bunker loopholed in a couple of places.'

'Make sure they have wide arcs of fire.'

'That's understood. Now,' Vogel went on, 'we shall be travelling in convoy to the airfield. There will be three cars, you and Professor Morrell in the middle car of the three.'

'My gun will never leave his head.'

'I'm well aware of that.' Vogel swallowed his bile. 'Your associate will do the driving of your car. We shall not approach you at any time.'

'I don't advise it.'

'It won't happen.' Vogel could not quite keep the asperity out of his voice. 'On arrival at the airfield, we shall take up station by the airport buildings. You will proceed in your car to the bunker. Professor Morrell will be held in the bunker while you check that everything about the plane is to your satisfaction.'

'Held at gun-point.'

'Yes,' said Vogel. 'I shan't forget that. Now we come to the actual exchange. I have no objection to what you propose. You seem to have thought things out very thoroughly, if I may say so.'

'Never mind the compliments.'

'You,' said Vogel, curling his lip, 'will signal by waving a white handkerchief. When we receive this signal, we shall send out the pilot, who will cross the field to join you in the bunker.'

'Under our guns. We have SLR's. We shouldn't miss.'

'Under your guns,' Vogel repeated submissively, grimacing with resentment. 'When the pilot is clearly in view, you will keep your part of the agreement and send out Professor Morrell. The two men will traverse the field at the same time but going in opposite directions.'

174

'Keep their routes separate. We want to be able to pick off either one of them if there's any funny business.'

'Understood. At the end of the transaction, you will have a pilot who will also act as hostage, and we shall have Professor Morrell. The pilot will take you to whatever destination you have in mind. We shan't try to stop that happening.'

'Better not. Unless you want the pilot's blood upon your conscience.'

Vogel bared his teeth. It was a smile of grim amusement. 'You have my word,' he promised.

'Parachutes,' came the voice. 'Don't forget them.'

'Parachutes will be supplied.'

'If we use them, the pilot goes out first.'

'They'll be in full working order.'

'That's it, then. We'll expect the cars tomorrow. Late afternoon, like I said.'

'Till tomorrow,' murmured Vogel. He put down the receiver. 'You bastard!' he added. Late afternoon, he thought. A flight into darkness. A light plane that could be put down almost anywhere. He reckoned he'd got the picture. He ran his tongue round his lips and scowled at the phone. It was not an interview he had much relished.

27

Arthur Morrell waited through the long hours of the next day with tension growing inside him. Moishe had told him about the deal. He knew that before nightfall he would either be free or lying dead with a bullet through his skull. Moishe had been embarrassed, telling him this. He had watched Moishe and Rachel clean their hand-guns and then do the same for the two elegant rifles with their telescopic sights. Time dragged by. Nobody could find anything to talk about. Moishe prowled about the room restlessly, but Rachel seemed to have entered a state of resigned calm.

In the late afternoon, a horn sounded and two black cars came rolling up the drive. The driver of the second car left his vehicle and climbed into the car in front, which drove immediately away. The big black limousine stood empty, awaiting them, outside the door.

Moishe untied the ropes round Morrell's ankles. 'Get up, Professor,' he said dourly. 'It's time to go.' He handed the rifles to Rachel, who slung one over each shoulder. When they reached the front door, Morrell felt his arm being grabbed and twisted up his back. Moishe stuck his ·38 up against Morrell's temple and Morrell could feel the muzzle, hard and cold, aching against the bone. 'Open the door now,' said Moishe to Rachel. Morrell found himself being pushed out first on to the steps and held there for a moment, the gun at his head, so as to make the position clear to anyone who might be observing them. Then he and Moishe walked awkwardly down the steps together and scrambled into the back seat of the car. Rachel followed, propping the rifles against the passenger seat and settling herself behind the wheel. She turned the key, the engine sprang to life, and they began to move. Once they were on the road, the guide car drew out ahead of them and another car took up station behind.

The three black cars moved sedately through the afternoon traffic. It was all too much like a funeral procession for Morrell's taste. He felt a desperate need to talk, to gain re-assurance from the familiar voices of the others, but Moishe and Rachel were obstinately silent now. They had withdrawn from him and he understood why. He realized that they chose to ignore him, to set him at a distance, because of what they might have to do to him before long. Moishe held the gun up hard against his ribs, close to his booming heart. Morrell tried to distract himself by looking out of the window. There were the shops, the people, men and women strolling on the pavements, following their ordinary lives. It was another world out there, one he felt he would never regain. It snatched at his heart like the memory of childhood. At the end of this, he would be an exile at best, and at worst a corpse. There must be love and happiness and trust in the world, but it seemed that none of it was for him. The deepest irony of all was that he felt closer to Moishe and Rachel now than to anybody else. Who were those men in the other cars? He did not know them. They were not friends who had come to his aid. No, they were mounting this rescue for other reasons than friendship. He was being saved because of the murderous knowledge he carried in his head. He was not a man to them, he was a walking formula, the blueprint of a doomsday weapon. It did not matter to them that the blueprint could suffer, that it might feel the pangs of betrayal, the hunger for love. All that was of no interest to them or their masters. There was a moment when Morrell wondered whether he might not be better dead, like the young man, David, but his body cringed at the idea. His body wanted to go on living. The flesh is the greatest coward, thought Morrell sadly. It bullies us into the deepest indignities, betrays us to all the worst things.

They had reached open country by now. The sun shone mildly upon turning leaves. It was a fading landscape, bidding its farewell to summer. They left the main road and took a secondary one, little more than a lane, that wound between tall hedgerows of beech. The car in front halted at a fork in the road where the left-hand turn was closed by a barrier. There were three workmen busy on the verges, and a sign showing a red arrow and the word 'Detour'. After a moment's discussion with the driver of the car in front, the workmen swung the barrier to one side, allowing the lead car to roll through. Rachel followed, and the third car held its station behind. The convoy was now moving on a route which was free from other traffic.

The airfield proved to be a modest affair: a couple of hangars, a low line of flat-roofed buildings and a few storage huts. There was just the one plane to be seen, standing at the far end of the strip, a white Comanche, looking lonely under the wide arch of the empty sky. A red-and-white wind-sock flapped sluggishly at the end of a pole, but apart from that nothing moved. Nor were there any people about. The place had a languishing, bereft air, like a ghost town.

Moishe spoke for the first time since they had begun their journey. 'Take the car straight out there,' he told Rachel in a tense voice. They left the tarmac and swayed forward over grass. Morrell watched the other cars go peeling away to disappear behind the hangars. How far was it? he wondered as they drew nearer to the gleaming Comanche. Three hundred yards? He knew about the walk he would have to make. Rachel stopped the car beside the bunker. It was an emplacement built entirely from sandbags, standing about seven feet high, each of its four walls a yard thick. It was open to the sky.

When they climbed out of the car, Moishe held the revolver up again to Morrell's head so that there should be no mistake. Morrell snatched a glance at the buildings in the distance. Between him and them there stretched a gulf of grass and asphalt, a flat plain, naked of cover. He thought he could make out the silhouettes of heads rising above the parapet on one side of the flat roofs. Of course, he thought. Their every movement would be closely watched.

Rachel followed them out of the car, bringing the rifles. Moishe drove Morrell in front of him towards the narrow opening which provided the entrance to the bunker. Once inside, Moishe kicked the sandbags as if to test them. 'They kept their word,' he said. 'So far.' He turned to Morrell and addressed him with remote cordiality. 'You're almost free, Professor. Don't go doing anything silly now.'

Morrell nodded. His mouth felt too dry for him to talk.

'Watch him a minute,' said Moishe to Rachel. 'I'll go check the plane.' He turned sternly to Morrell. 'Don't make any trouble.'

'Moishe,' said Morrell, his voice clogged, 'you can trust me. Surely you know that?'

'Well . . .' Moishe shrugged and went out of the bunker.

Morrell was left alone with Rachel. She gave him a remote stare. She seemed very young to Morrell at that moment, young and frail, with a shadowed, wounded beauty in her face.

'I only wish I could tell you . . .' he began.

'Don't talk,' said Rachel. 'Just don't say anything.' The gun remained steady in her hand.

'Then don't hate me,' pleaded Morrell. 'Don't blame me, Rachel.'

She shook her head. Her brilliant dark eyes looked through him, beyond him, to some place where he counted for nothing.

They stood in silence till Moishe returned.

'Everything's OK,' said Moishe. 'They've kept their word.' He gave Morrell a flashing, strained smile. 'Patience now, Professor. Your turn is coming. We're about to make the swap.' He put a rifle ready in each of the embrasures. 'But don't forget, you'll be in our sights all the way.' Moishe gave an apologetic shrug. 'It's a sad state of affairs, Professor, but I find I still have to threaten you. I have to do it right to the end.' Moishe took a white handkerchief from his pocket and fluttered it through the embrasure. 'Now,' he said thoughtfully.

'Now?' echoed Morrell. He began to walk towards the entrance of the bunker.

'Not yet,' said Moishe, grinning. 'Don't be too eager, Professor. First the pilot must be on his way. When the time comes, I'll point you in the right direction. Don't stray from it, Professor. That's important.' He put out a big hand. 'No hard feelings? Well, not too many, huh?' he added with a wry grin.

Morrell gripped the hand with his own. 'None,' he blurted, 'none,' embarrassed by the eagerness of his voice.

'Don't be so sure,' said Moishe. 'Maybe you'll change your mind when I have to shoot you in the back.'

Morrell turned his face away as if he had been struck.

Moishe saw the movement and understood it. 'That's not going to happen, Professor,' he said. 'Regard it as a joke on my part. A joke in poor taste. You'll be OK.'

'Look!' cried Rachel, pointing through the embrasure.

A distant figure in a blue uniform had begun making his way towards them over the open ground.

28

It had been a strange, disquieting day for Roper, a day filled with painful pleasure, a day on which he remembered Hamid very often. He knew how it must end. Here, before him, lay the candidate, the sacrifice to be combed and garlanded. Staring at the body, Roper was troubled by conflicting desires. He had lived all day among the fearful ambiguities of his heart.

Roper had insisted on doing with his own hands all that had to be done. He had been alone for hours with the body. He had stripped it tenderly and let his fingers move over the slim flanks, the buttocks marred only by the puncture where the dart had gone in. He had even rubbed ointment on to the wound, but before that, he had washed the young man from head to foot, poring over the body, mapping it with his eyes, making it over to himself. He wanted to know this body, to be familiar with its beauty before he gave it to destruction.

Vogel had come in and surprised him at his task, and the American had turned away in disgust after looking into his face. Roper did not care. He understood Vogel's feelings but they left him cold. Vogel, he thought, is only a monster of a different kind. Vogel is a man for nauseas, a frigid ideologist, all his virtues rooted in repugnance. He reckoned he had Vogel's number. We are all monsters of one sort or another, thought Roper. He was aware that Vogel's tolerance of him was wearing thin. The idea rather pleased him. All the same, he had to admit the ingenuity of the scheme. It was Vogel's baby. Vogel had thought it up and Vogel had taken the risks. He had come through the really dangerous time and was now well on course for a triumphant demonstration of Vogel's Third Law. Roper felt a shiver of anticipation at the idea, though at the same time it depressed him.

He looked into the young man's face and thought, If only life could be simple, if only the complicated hungers would let him be. But Roper knew that, for him, too close an approach to simplicity would be an approach to death. He also knew that death was coming for him – though not today. It was not his turn yet. Today he would watch others die. He would be part of the excitement, the drama of deceit.

Roper touched the young man's cheek. He really was very like Hamid : the same oval face, the black locks tumbling across the forehead, the slender physique. Curious to think that in life they would have been enemies. Hamid had been an Arab and it seemed this one was a Jew. At least, he was reported to have called on a rabbi, so presumably he was a Jew. Roper could not understand why a Jewish terrorist would risk his life trying to kidnap an American scientist. He would have liked to interrogate the young man but that was not going to be possible.

Roper took hot water and a shaving-brush and worked lather gently into the young man's moustache. A few minutes' work with a razor and the moustache was gone. His hair, thought Roper. What colour shall that be? The contrast ought to be as striking as possible, so that meant settling for yellow or red. He chose red.

'Judas-coloured hair for you,' said Roper, 'because that's going to be your role. An unknowing Judas, an ignorant Judas, but a Judas all the same.' Roper applied the dye to the hair and eyebrows. He was deft and painstaking, standing back from time to time to admire the effect.

The young man stirred.

Roper looked at his watch. The last dosage would almost have worn off by now. Soon the man would awaken and the finale could begin. It was time to dress him for the part. Roper bade goodbye with regret to the young man's nakedness. It was so fine, the physique so moving, so slender, the skin without a blemish except for the puncture high on the left buttock where Vogel's tranquillizing dart had entered. Oh clever, Vogel! though Roper. Clever! Vogel would redeem himself with this day's work. He shook his head and began to pull the trousers up over the young man's legs. After the trousers came the shirt, then the tunic, the socks, the shoes. It is never easy to dress an unconscious man, but Roper applied himself to the task with assiduous care.

Pearson came in to tell him he had received word that they were on their way.

'Well, what do you think?' asked Roper, gesturing to the red-headed man in the pilot's uniform who lay on the table. He was beginning to stir now, as if his sleep had been broken by the sound of their voices.

'It's quite a transformation,' said Pearson, and gave a flustered laugh. 'I'd better get back to my post, I guess.' He was uneasy with Roper, a little unnerved by him.

'You've done as I asked?' said Roper.

'Yeah. No mirrors, no reflecting surfaces. We've even dulled down the glass partitions in the corridor.'

'Splendid!'

Pearson left.

Roper took from his pocket a small plastic bottle fitted with a rubber teat. He squeezed drops of a colourless liquid into the corners of the young man's eyes. 'Tears,' he murmured. 'Roper's gift.'

The young man opened his eyes and blinked rapidly at the ceiling. Roper leant over him, smiling. He watched the brown eyes struggle to focus. They were pools of bewilderment, brimming with moisture. The eyes closed again. How long and dark the lashes were, wet against the cheeks!

Vogel put in another appearance. 'How is it, Roper?'

'He's just coming round. Be with us in a minute.'

Vogel had a hungry look. The arches of his nostrils were pinched and bloodless.

'They're about to hit the field,' he said, his voice guarded.

'Well, maestro,' said Roper. 'So your cunning has not deserted you.'

'Cut the crap.' Vogel stared at the young man in the pilot's uniform. 'You've done a good job on him, I'll say that, Roper.'

'Yours were the brains,' said Roper. 'I was only the humble instrument.'

'Yeah,' said Vogel with distaste. 'I *saw* what you were.' He heard the young man begin to mutter and went on quickly: 'We talk nicely to him, Roper. He'll be disorientated. We keep him that way. We have to talk nice. He'll be malleable, but it must be done quick. He'll swallow it, if it's put to him right.'

'Don't worry,' said Roper. 'Leave this to me: it's my speciality, Vogel. My field.'

'Hmm,' said Vogel. 'Well, the sooner the better.'

'Five minutes, Vogel. Just five minutes' gentle persuasion.'

Vogel grunted. 'See you out there with our pilot.' He found a cold smile for Roper and left to make his final dispositions.

'Sure,' said Roper softly. 'We'll be there, my friend and I.'

'What's going on?' asked the young man in a dazed voice. 'Where am I, please?'

Roper went and helped him to sit up. 'It's all right,' he said. 'Just listen and I'll tell you . . .'

David was walking across the grass. He could not see very well, his eyes kept watering, but he was able to make out the white shape of the plane and the emplacement in front of it. There, too, was the stockade of sandbags. The scene was just as the man had described it. He felt he could trust the man. Rachel would be in the bunker, Rachel and Moishe. His heart filled with joy at the prospect of seeing them again. The man had not been hostile, not considering he was one of their opponents. He admitted that they had won, and he was not angry at all. He explained how David had knocked himself unconscious when he fell and that since then he'd been suffering from concussion. The man praised Rachel and Moishe for their loyalty to him. David lingered over the man's words. Rachel and Moishe had insisted on his return. They had made it an essential part of any deal. They had gone to great lengths, according to the man, risking themselves to take more hostages in order to ensure they got him back. '*Chaverim*,' he murmured. There they were, waiting for him, and there was the plane that would take them all to safety. How would it be? wondered David bemusedly. His head was ringing and he found it hard to think. Moishe would have worked everything out, he told himself. It came back into his mind that they had won. Their plan had worked! He felt a huge wave of elation. He would have liked to run to the emplacement, but the man had impressed it upon him that he should walk steadily so as not to cause alarm. There must be no risk of an accident. Best to do as he said.

David trudged over the flat plain of the field, his heart burning with impatience. He saw another figure some distance away, moving in the opposite direction. Yes, that was right. That would be the exchange. It should be Professor Morrell. He peered at the figure through swimming eyes and thought he recognized the greying hair, the big frame. It was all going exactly as the man had said. Oh *chaverim*! he thought. My people, my country! Rachel, my dear love!

It was not much farther now.

Moishe and Rachel leant in the embrasures, their rifles against their shoulders. Moishe sighted on the retreating back of Professor Morrell. He held him easily between the crossed hairs and could have brought him down without any trouble, but he did not believe it was going to be demanded of him now. He would be spared that. He would not have liked shooting Morrell. It was hard to kill a man you knew. Every now and then, Moishe glanced quickly across to his right to check on the progress of the pilot. The man was plodding forward without much enthusiasm, but that was understandable. He was a thin, red-haired man, dressed in a blue uniform, his peaked cap worn slightly awry, like a token of his nervousness. But a brave fellow, all the same, thought Moishe. He wondered what sort of man the pilot would be – not that it mattered, so long as he flew the plane. Moishe brought his attention back to Morrell; it was Rachel's job to cover the pilot. He did not doubt her willingness to shoot if there were any attempt at trickery. Rachel was in a harsh, courageous mood, but Moishe did not expect that it would last. He saw it as her way of fending off grief. She had postponed her time of mourning but she would have to go through it later. Once they were in Holland, she would be looked after by the group in Amsterdam. It would be necessary to lie low for a while and Moishe vowed he would help Rachel through her sorrow. He felt that this was not beyond him any more. As for the escape, they needed only moderate luck . . . A plane like the Comanche could be put down almost anywhere, a field, an empty road. Once that was done, they could get clear of it in no time. By tomorrow they should be established at a safe house in Amsterdam. A couple more minutes and the exchange would be completed. Moishe felt eager to wrap the business up and be gone.

Rachel was watching the pilot approaching. She held her gun on him without wavering, but as he drew nearer she felt uneasiness take hold of her. There was something strangely familiar about the man's walk. She peered hard at him. His hair was the wrong colour and he had no moustache but he looked . . . she swallowed hard . . . he looked like David. She bit her lip and closed her eyes against the sight of the man. It was a grotesque joke that the pilot should be so like David. She did not think she could stand it. She drooped her head miserably over the gun. Am I going crazy? she thought. Am I as bad as that? Shall I keep on thinking I see him, wherever I go in the world? Is that what's going to happen? Is that the future for me? Oh, it would be beyond bearing! She fought hard to keep control. She knew she must not break down now. When I look again, she told herself, I shall see that all this is only my imagination. The pilot was much nearer now. She lifted her head and stared at him through the sights. God, God, it was worse than ever! The likeness was

even stronger than before. If it had not been for the hair . . .
Rachel felt tears smarting at the corners of her eyes. This was
all too cruel. She looked into the man's face from only twenty
yards away and a loud cry broke from her lips.

Vogel was standing on the flat roof under cover of the parapet
with Roper beside him. Pearson was a little farther along,
nursing an SLR. A couple more armed men were crouched on
the roof, but they were only a back-up. The outcome of the
action did not depend on them. Vogel and Roper watched
the two figures cross the open ground. They looked small and
ordinary, the grass stretching away on all sides of them. This
was the amphitheatre before the show began. The martyrs
were not yet tied to their stakes. Roper sniffed the air. It
seemed heavy. There was a chill in it, a taste like fog.
    'Nearly time,' said Vogel. He had decided on one final
precaution, and now was the time to put it into action.
    'Run out the screen,' he said and gave the signal. The roar
of an engine sounded and an armoured Land-Rover hurtled
out of the shadows of the hangar. Within a few seconds it had
put itself between Morrell and the bunker, which meant that
Morrell was no longer a target. Vogel watched with grave
pleasure as the driver flung himself out of the cab and hustled
Morrell away to safety. Vogel had judged Morrell to be
slightly vulnerable in the last stages of the exchange. It was
just possible that the terrorists might not only recognize the
pilot as their dead associate, but be able to grasp the full
import of his appearance and strike back. Possible, but very
unlikely. Vogel guessed they would be too bewildered, thrown
by the impossibility of the thing, unable to work out the
implications. All the same, Vogel had guarded against the
chance of retaliation. The armoured Land-Rover was an
insurance, and it had worked. Vogel gave a sigh of satisfaction.
Morrell had been gathered into the fold. He was safe. Now the
other matter could go forward.
    'Can you take him?' Vogel called lightly to Pearson. He
pointed to the figure in the blue uniform. The man was

running the last few yards to the bunker. Pearson hefted the rifle and settled it into his shoulder.

'Ten dollars says you don't,' Vogel added, with a smile.

The sudden roaring and screeching of the engine brought David's head round, and when he saw the Land-Rover, panic awoke in him. The Land-Rover seemed to be heading right towards him, and he was so close to the bunker now, he could not abide the thought that anything might go wrong. Then he heard Rachel's voice and he started to run. As he swung round the corner of the bunker one of the sandbags split open and sand spurted into the air. He heard the report a moment later, just as he stumbled through the entrance.

'Rachel!' he said, panting. 'Moishe! Here I am!' He spread his arms wide to them.

They stood staring, motionless, consternation on their faces. Then Rachel gave a cry and ran to embrace him. David surrendered himself to her arms. He heard her voice, wild and trembling, saying strange things. 'Oh, my darling,' she was saying. 'You're alive. Oh, David, David. What have they done to you? David, you're back with us, you're alive. We're together again.' Her mouth pressed against his lips, his cheeks were wet by her tears, he smelt the familiar fragrance of her hair, and yet in the midst of all this tumult of happiness he seemed to hear the first footfall of enormity. Something somehow was dreadfully wrong.

Moishe watched David and Rachel embrace each other. He bowed his head and let the storm of their joy roll over him. Such desperate happiness as had befallen Rachel was granted to very few people. Let her enjoy it. Let her cup brim, let it run over. Let her drain it while she could, let her die with the sweetness on her tongue. There would be no more chances. They were finished. Moishe was certain of it. He felt bitter, not at the approach of death, but from the realization that he had been tricked, out-manœuvred. He snatched up the rifle and sent a couple of rounds thudding fiercely against the armour of the Land-Rover.

Rachel and David broke off their embrace.

'Where are the others?' said David.

'Others? We are all here, cousin.'

'I mean, the other hostages?'

Moishe shrugged slowly and waved his hands round the corners of the bunker. 'You see them.'

'But he told me . . .' David's voice shook and then faltered into silence. 'I believed him,' he began again, more calmly. 'I'm to blame for this mess.'

'No,' said Moishe. 'And in any case, it doesn't matter.'

'What are we going to do?' asked Rachel. She looked at Moishe as if she thought he might still have some answer.

'The plane . . . ?' said David wildly. 'Could we . . . ?'

'Who is flying the plane? We have lost our pilot. Besides, we wouldn't get a yard.'

'What then? Do we . . . surrender?' faltered Rachel.

'Surrender? They aren't going to let us surrender, kids. They haven't gone to all this trouble so that we can just surrender.'

It was a bad moment for them all.

'Fight, then?' said David. His voice made it clear that he understood. He put an arm round Rachel.

'Pray,' said Moishe lightly. 'Praying might be better.'

'Don't mock us, cousin. Not now.'

'I mean it,' said Moishe, a harsh gaiety appearing in his voice. He looked at these two forlorn children who were destined to be his companions in death and was glad to have their company, though he longed to stir their hearts. He would have liked them to go out in obstinacy and pride.

'You know what my father told me?' said Moishe. 'You know what he told me when he was dying? "Don't be sad," said my old man. "I'm being called to a great occasion. I'm going to the Sabbath meal in Heaven, Moishe. For fish we will eat Leviathan, and for meat we shall have the Ox of the Desert. Our wine will be the best – pressed from the grapes of Eden." ' Moishe began to laugh at the memory. 'So be glad,' he said. 'There is a good time coming. Give thanks, kids.' Moishe paused. 'Well, we've already feasted off one sort of Leviathan. Now comes the big fish.' He opened his arms wide and laughed.

Rachel and David looked at him with startled hope. His laughter encouraged them to smile back.

And then the bombardment began.

Roper felt the thrill, the profound awesome reverberations echoing in the caves of his body, and then, soon after, the expected coldness settled round his heart. They were using grenade-launchers fitted to SLR rifles. The grenades sailed through the sky in leisurely arcs. When they exploded, huge sprays of sand fanned upwards, like storm waves breaking upon rocks. Tatters of canvas were slung into the air. Rags, thought Roper. Everything goes to rags. The bunker melted before his eyes. Through the smoke, he could see it foundering into ruin. A grenade must have struck the Comanche. There was a sudden leap of flame and then black oily smoke rolled over the bunker, covering it like a pall.

The bombardment went on and on. Roper glanced across at Vogel. The American's face remained inscrutable. That's enough, thought Roper. They must be blown to bits by now. Their flesh will be in rags. He thought of Hamid, cut down by the Sten, and the young man naked on the table. That body, too, would be ruined now. Broken. I am definitely not fit to live, thought Roper, but with the knowledge there came a furtive pleasure. While that remained, he would not die.

Suddenly Morrell appeared beside them, shouting and bawling. 'They're still inside,' Morrell kept yelling, as if they couldn't possibly know, as if there must be some profound misreading of the situation on their part.

Vogel gave him an even stare. 'Glad to have you back with us, Professor.'

'You must order them to stop. Don't you realize . . . ?'

'Sure.' Vogel gave a nod. 'Hold your fire,' he called.

A huge silence descended.

Black smoke rolled over the bunker.

I am still alive, thought Moishe. There must be some mistake. Death had roared in his face like a lion, yet it had not struck him down. He tried to push away the sandbags that had fallen across him but found that his left arm did not work. It dangled from his shoulder like a length of rope. He struggled free as best he could. There was a jagged wound where shrapnel had ripped his thigh open and blood was streaming down his leg. He peered through the smoke and saw David and Rachel lying tangled together like two smashed dolls. They had gone first. Now it must be his turn.

Moishe's ears ached in the new silence. It looked as if death were shy of him and he would have to go out there and find it. He picked up the twisted ruin of his rifle and tossed it aside. He still had the ·38. He took it in his good hand and began to lurch forward. His shoe squelched. It was full of blood. He walked towards the airport buildings, and as he cleared the black smoke, he held his good arm up; he waved his arm and shouted to capture death's attention. He found himself repeating words that had lingered in his head from before the brutal roaring overwhelmed them all.

'Look!' said Roper.

Out of the smoke there came a blackened, bleeding figure, reeling like a drunk, waving his arms and babbling strange phrases.

'Feast on Leviathan,' cried the figure. 'Booze on the wine of Eden. Doesn't that appeal? Come on, gentlemen. Let's make a fight of it. Does nobody want to get to eat the big fish with me?' He laughed as if he had made a good joke, then fired his gun towards the airport buildings before staggering on.

We touched you, Moishe was thinking. We reached out and got to you. We did that, you power-mongers. You shakers of nations. We knocked one of you over. That's not bad going for two greenhorns and a has-been.

'Come on, you bastards!' he yelled. 'Finish this.'

And I know, thought Moishe, that when death comes, the one who pulls the trigger will not be the man who ordered the bullet to be fired. That man won't be around.

'What's the matter with you all?' he bellowed. 'Has everyone gone home?' He was tottering now, weaving back and forth, the damaged leg giving way under him.

Somewhere out there, thought Moishe, there will be a cat, and the cat will be sleeping.

That was the truth about this world.

The marksmen waited for orders. Vogel was staring at the advancing scarecrow. He seemed hypnotized by the man's ravings. Finally Pearson said, 'How about it, Chief? Do we take him or don't we?'

'We take him,' drawled Vogel. 'No,' he added, as Pearson began to raise his rifle. '*I* take him.' He held out his hand.

Pearson shrugged and passed him the gun.

Vogel took precise aim.

'You can't do that!' It was Morrell, tugging at his arm. The scientist loomed at him, a flabby face, the eyes staring.

Vogel gestured for Pearson to restrain Morrell.

'Don't you see?' shouted Morrell, struggling vainly to break free. 'Moishe's trying to give himself up!'

'The man is armed,' said Vogel. He was still listening to the terrorist's ravings, fascinated by the strangeness and passion of the words. It was one way of facing death, thought Vogel. The man had got himself drunk on words for it, like a poet. He found the terrorist in the sights, fixed his forehead at the junction of the crossed hairs. It was the hair-haired one. How close he looked! I will give you a clean death, thought Vogel. That is a great privilege for a human being. That is magnanimity.

The man seemed to sense Vogel's intention. He stood still and thrust his head forward. Vogel found he was not entirely happy with the task. This is the man who killed Garen, he reminded himself, but he could not see it as either justice or revenge. When you do this, he told himself, you are a tool like Garen. You are Garen's heir.

The brutal face loomed at him, sneering. He seemed to have Garen in the sights, and when he squeezed the trigger it was Garen he shot.

Moishe tumbled over and lay still.

'No need,' Morrell kept saying brokenly. 'No call,' and he began to sob.

Vogel turned to him. 'There is a plane waiting for you, Professor Morrell, a private plane, and I have orders to get you on it as soon as possible. You see how important you are, Professor? They've given you a plane all to yourself. They're very keen to have you back in the States.'

'Why did you do it?' said Morrell. 'Why? When he was no threat?'

'Take the plane, Professor.'

'*Why?*'

Vogel looked at the weakly handsome face, the petulant mouth. All this for you, he thought grudgingly. 'You've had a hard ride, Professor,' he said, holding his voice even. 'You shouldn't bother your head with these questions – Pearson, take a couple of officers and escort Professor Morrell to his plane. Look after him well. He's worth a lot.'

As he left, Morrell cast Vogel a haggard, appalled glance.

'Professor,' called Vogel. 'You just don't understand.'

'And you?' came Roper's voice. 'What about you, Vogel? Do you understand?'

'I don't need to understand.'

'Orders?' Roper made a sneer out of the word.

'That's right, Roper. Orders. You know the score. We all work on the same basis.'

'Say it for me, Vogel. Say it!'

'Restricted access. No more should be disclosed to an officer than he needs to know for the performance of his duties. It makes good sense, Roper.'

'And you reckon we were told *enough*?'

Vogel fixed Roper with a hostile stare. 'Are you trying to take another rise out of me?'

'I shouldn't think you've got a rise in you, Vogel.' Roper pointed to Moishe's corpse. 'But you enjoyed doing that. I saw you, Vogel. You're a natural butcher. A cold-hearted mean son of a bitch.'

'Don't hang any more of your queen's talk on me, Roper. I've stood all I can of that.' He paused. 'It was a clean kill.'

'There speaks the mighty hunter,' said Roper venomously.

'If you have any criticism to make of my conduct in this operation . . .'

'It's not the operation, Vogel. It's you.'

Vogel waited, challenging Roper to go on.

'You know what's wrong with you, Vogel. You don't *suffer* enough.'

The two men confronted each other. As soon as the game was over, their natural antipathy came out into the open.

Vogel shrugged. 'It'll need to be a joint report.'

'You write it,' said Roper. 'You're the one who understands.'

Vogel made a last effort. 'We're bound to be a little frayed right now. Let's not part on bad terms. I'll see you around.'

'I'll see you in hell, General!'

'Not your hell,' snarled Vogel. 'According to Dante, sodomites have their own stinking circle.'

Roper gave a maddening, derisive whinny: 'Go on, say it, Vogel. You wouldn't be seen dead in *my* hell!' He waved a big white hand in farewell. 'Pleasure working with you, General, I must say.'

'Fuck off!' retorted Vogel, as brutally as he knew how.

'Thanks,' said Roper with a sigh. 'That's better.'

Vogel turned his head and when he looked again, Roper had gone.

'All right!' called Vogel to his men. 'Let's get this trash cleared up.' He waved towards the gutted plane, the broken bunker, the dead. 'I want it put absolutely to rights.' Vogel closed his eyes and called to mind the African plains: clean, empty spaces with only the great beasts roaming there, innocent creatures incapable of sin. 'Let's put the wraps on this bloody business.'

29

Next day a short report appeared in a few English newspapers. It described the attempt of three unidentified terrorists to seize a Piper Comanche from a private airfield in Hampshire. According to the report, the terrorists died when the plane they had seized exploded on the ground, blown up by the accidental detonation of a grenade they were carrying. The motives of the terrorists were described as obscure, but the suggestion was tentatively put forward that these might have been the same people who had planted the bomb in the Oxford Street Underground two days earlier.

The account was given very little space. It was almost crowded off the page by the columns of print devoted to the latest detailed reports from Washington concerning the fall of the Secretary of State. Only a couple of men in the world could make the connection between these two events, and neither of them was going to do any talking.

The truth would never get into the history books.